He Hadn't Wanted To Hurt Peg.

He'd just wanted to kiss her. Just once, for old times' sake. Just once, to see if his memory had been bigger than the reality.

Now he knew. His memory didn't even begin to compare with the real-life perfection of Peg Lathrop's lips. Or her long, lithe body pressed against his like a firebrand. Or the softness of her breasts warm and heavy in his hands.

Well, so much for what he'd wanted, he decided. He'd go for a ride with Peg and her little cowgirl—because he'd promised that he would. Then he'd get out of Dodge. Now that he knew he'd hurt Peg six years ago, he didn't want to hurt her again. And if he stuck around much longer, that's just what he'd do. He'd hurt her because now he knew something else. Something that he hadn't known before.

He wanted more from Peg than a kiss....

Dear Reader,

This season of harvest brings a cornucopia of six new passionate, powerful and provocative love stories from Silhouette Desire for your enjoyment.

Don't miss our current MAN OF THE MONTH title, Cindy Gerard's *Taming the Outlaw,* a reunion romance featuring a cowboy dealing with the unexpected consequences of a hometown summer of passion. And of course you'll want to read Katherine Garbera's *Cinderella's Convenient Husband,* the tenth absorbing title in Silhouette Desire's DYNASTIES: THE CONNELLYS continuity series.

A Navy SEAL is on a mission to win the love of the woman he left behind, in *The SEAL's Surprise Baby* by Amy J. Fetzer, while a TV anchorwoman gets up close and personal with a high-ranking soldier in *The Royal Treatment* by Maureen Child. This is the latest title in the exciting Silhouette crossline series CROWN AND GLORY.

Opposites attract when a sexy hunk and a matchmaker share digs in *Hearts Are Wild* by Laura Wright. And in *Secrets, Lies and...Passion* by Linda Conrad, a single mom is drawn into a web of desire and danger by the lover who jilted her at the altar years before...or did he?

Experience all six of these sensuous romances from Silhouette Desire this month, and guarantee that your Halloween will be all treat, no trick.

Enjoy!

Joan Marlow Golan

Joan Marlow Golan
Senior Editor, Silhouette Desire

Please address questions and book requests to:
Silhouette Reader Service
U.S.: 3010 Walden Ave., P.O. Box 1325, Buffalo, NY 14269
Canadian: P.O. Box 609, Fort Erie, Ont. L2A 5X3

Taming the Outlaw

CINDY GERARD

Published by Silhouette Books
America's Publisher of Contemporary Romance

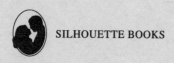 SILHOUETTE BOOKS

ISBN 0-373-76465-0

TAMING THE OUTLAW

Printed in U.S.A.

CINDY GERARD

If asked "What's your idea of heaven?" Cindy Gerard would say a warm sun, a cool breeze, pan pizza and a good book. If she had to settle for one of the four, she'd opt for the book, with the pizza running a close second. Inspired by the pleasure she's received from the books she's read and her longtime love affair with her husband, Tom, Cindy now creates her own evocative and sensual love stories about compelling characters and complex relationships.

This bestselling author of close to twenty books has received numerous industry awards, among them the National Readers' Choice Award, multiple *Romantic Times* nominations and two RITA® Award nominations from the Romance Writers of America. Cindy loves to hear from her readers and invites them to visit her Web page at www.tlt.com/authors/cgerard.htm.

This book is dedicated to Kyle and Eileen Gerard
for being you and for the gift of Kayla Marie,
sweet child, who owns me, heart and soul.

One

When Cutter Reno drifted out of Sundown, Montana, six years ago, he'd always figured he'd be back someday. He had friends here. He had memories here, some good, some not so good. And he supposed, in the overall scheme of things, Sundown came as close to "home" as any place he'd landed in his twenty-six years.

What he hadn't figured on was that when he did finally make an appearance it would be as the grand marshall of the annual Fourth of July parade.

Guess that goes to show how much he knew. He'd never counted on winning back-to-back National PRCA saddle bronc championships, either. And as it turned out, it was the celebrity status of the championships that had prompted his old buddy, Sam Perkins, to track him down and asked him to come back to lead the parade.

He shifted in the saddle and smiled at the faces lining the street. Then he tried not to think about the competitions and the money he was missing out on.

"Half the county will turn out to see you in the parade tomorrow," Sam had told him last night when they'd gotten together at the Dusk to Dawn Bar to catch up. "Why, it's downright huge."

By Sundown, Montana, population four hundred and seventy-three, standards, Cutter supposed it was a pretty big deal. Close as he could figure, it was four blocks long—a new record according to Sam—as it snaked with dogged enthusiasm along the length of Main Street strung with red, white and blue banners. Among the highlights was a twenty-one piece all-school marching band.

"Yeah, we'd a' had twenty-two marchers if Billy Capper hadn't busted his nose in the softball game yesterday when his face connected with Joe Gillman's bat." This from Snake Gibson, a barrel-chested old wrangler who'd joined in on the bull-slinging at the bar last night.

The consensus, over cold longnecks and shelled peanuts, was that since Sundown had beaten neighboring Shueyville in a ninth-inning squeaker, Billy's absence would be missed but not overly mourned.

The band seemed to be holding their own without him, too, Cutter thought, as they sweltered in their red wool uniforms, desperately tried to keep close ranks and belt out a Sousa march. It was a shame they were working so hard, though, because for all their efforts, he was a little embarrassed to discover that all eyes were turned on him.

Well, almost all eyes, Cutter conceded as he spotted a six-year-old memory that should have worked its way out of his system by now. The moment he saw Peg Lathrop, Cutter lost all awareness of the summer sun beating down, burning through his gray-and-black plaid shirt.

The band, the laughter and the cheers from the crowd all faded to background noise as Cutter shifted to autopilot, automatically reining in the big bay gelding when it crow-hopped away from an escaped red balloon. He was only aware of the chestnut-haired woman who moved purposefully along the fringe of the route, avoiding his gaze like she was practicing a religion.

''Ain't he just the cat's meow.''

Peg Lathrop crossed her arms beneath her breasts and gave her friend, Krystal Perkins, a tight smile. ''Well, you've got the cat part right. What he is, is what he always was—an alley cat with an attitude.''

Didn't look like he'd changed a bit, either, Peg decided, watching him wave to the cheering crowd from astride the big gelding the parade committee had arranged for him to ride. With effort, she schooled her gaze away from Cutter Reno's lean rangy angles and slow, seductive grins. Then she told herself that seeing him again didn't hurt. She wasn't angry with him anymore, either. It might have been easier to forgive him, though, if he hadn't known exactly what effect he had on women. Just like he knew exactly what result he was after. Lay 'em and leave 'em.

"Would ya just look at him?" Krystal continued, shaking her head in awe. "Lord above but he's pretty."

Peg had been trying not to look. She straightened her shoulders and scowled at Krystal whose turned-up nose, flashing green eyes and short brown hair had a tendency to make people dismiss her as flighty when in fact she was as grounded as an oak. She was also the most happily married woman Peg knew.

"Sam catches you drooling over Reno like that and you may be looking for an alley to sleep in yourself."

Krystal laughed and hiked her ice-cream-cone-wielding two-year-old son, Grant, higher on her hip. "No crime in lookin' at the package," she said, as Grant smeared chocolate ice cream from his chin to his chest and gave his momma a sticky smile. "As long as the only place I go lookin' for love is with the little guy's daddy here, right baby boy?"

The reference to his father had Grant warming to his current favorite phrase. "Where Daddy go? Where Daddy go?" His brown eyes danced as he bounced on his momma's hip, making a game of it.

"Daddy's on the fire truck, punkin'. You watch. He'll be comin' along pretty soon now. And Momma will just watch that ole alley cat till Daddy gets here, okay?"

Peg snorted. "You make sure you grow up to be like your daddy, Grant." She patted the little boy's back with affection. "Good men like him are hard to find."

And even harder to keep, she thought as her gaze involuntarily sought, then connected with the stunning brilliance of Cutter Reno's slashing smile.

Peg froze the moment their gazes caught and held. As Grant continued to chatter in the background, she felt the warming pleasure in Cutter's summer-blue eyes—and the rabbit-run beat of her heart as it kicked up and thumped her in the chest.

Tearing her gaze away, she gripped her five-year-old daughter's hand tightly in hers and told herself she wasn't running. "Come on, Shell. I see Grampa Jack. Let's go find out if he's got a spot picked out to watch the fireworks tonight."

"But I wanna see the rest of the parade," Shelby protested, planting her tiny scuffed red cowboy boots on the sun-softened asphalt.

Peg looked down at her very own grubby little rainbow. The fine blond hair peeking out beneath her lavender cowboy hat was damp and curling with sweat and escaping in little wisps from twin Annie Oakley braids. Her yellow sunsuit was stained with the same chocolate ice cream as Grant's shirt; her cherub face was pink from the sun and the heat and flushed with excitement. Startlingly blue eyes sparkled with stubborn determination.

"I bet you can see it better from Grampa's shoulders."

Peg knew she'd won the point when Shelby made a beeline for Jack Lathrop who was standing with a group of his cronies at the end of the block.

"Say goodbye to Krystal and Grant," Peg chastised with a shake of her head.

"Bye Krystal. Bye Grant," Shelby called over her shoulder as she loped toward her grandpa.

Peg rolled her eyes then smiled an apology at Krystal. Her smile faded at her friend's speculative frown. "What?"

"Have you decided yet if you're going to see him?" Like her voice, Krystal's eyes were soft.

Peg looked at her sandaled feet, studied the siren-red nail polish on her toes. There was no point in playing coy. Ever since Krystal's husband, Sam, who'd chaired the parade committee, had happily reported that his buddy, Cutter Reno, had agreed to be this year's grand marshall, Krystal had been after her. "Not if I can help it."

Krystal's frown changed from concerned to admonishing.

"Got to go," Peg said before Krystal could launch into a minilecture on why she should talk to Cutter.

"Okay," Krystal conceded at Peg's closed-off look. "No more questions—at least about Cutter, but are we still on for the picnic tonight before the fireworks?"

Peg narrowed her eyes. "Cutter going to be there?"

With her gaze intent on Peg, Krystal nodded.

"Then I'll skip that particular party, thanks."

"Peg—"

"—Don't. Don't say it," Peg cut in, then felt ashamed for snapping. She held up her hand. "Sorry. Just let it go, okay? I've got to deal with this the way I think is best."

Before the conversation escalated into something

she couldn't keep up with, she gave Grant a peck on the cheek and Krystal a one-armed hug. "Maybe I'll see you tonight at the fireworks. Thanks for watching Shell this morning."

Studiously avoiding the cowboy on the horse in the black hat and tight jeans, she threaded her way through the crowd toward the little girl whose hand was linked with the man Peg called Daddy and Shelby called Grandpa. Then she assured herself that Cutter would be gone tomorrow and life, like her heartbeat, would settle back to normal.

Pretty Peggy Lathrop. Man, Cutter thought as he watched her move along the parade route. She always had been a fine sight. Time had only improved on the package of sleek lines and knockout curves. Paint-tight blue jean cutoffs showed off slim hips and long tan legs. A tiny white spaghetti strap tank top hugged a pair of unbelievably lush breasts. The hint of a tanned tummy peeked between the scrap of stretchy cotton and the waistband of those hip-hugging shorts.

As his horse plodded along at parade speed, he did his damnedest to keep a bead on her. Beneath a pale straw Stetson that partially shaded her face, a length of satin straight hair fell to nearly her waist. The July sun glinted off the shining mass, setting off flashes of light like a prairie fire. When he finally got around to checking out the face her hat brim shadowed, he was just as taken as he was with the rest of her—and got pleasantly lost in a sweet summer memory of long-legged Peg.

Pretty little brown-eyed girl.

Never taking his eyes off her, he lifted his hat, re-settled it, and with a smile of pure pleasure, prepared to get sentimentally sappy over the fire of an old flame that had never quite burned itself out. They'd had a little thing six years ago. It had been the summer of his sophomore year in the PRCA. He'd been flying high, still pumped up over being named Rookie of the Year. He'd come home to Sundown a hero then, too. And he'd found little Peg all grown up. When he left town again, he'd left a winner in more ways than one.

Still watching her, he shifted the reins to his left hand, absently rubbed the flat of his palm along his thigh. There was no way she didn't remember. He'd seen it in her eyes in the brief moment when their gazes had connected over the crowd. He'd waited for her to smile for him. Instead, she'd looked away faster than the swish of the gelding's tail.

He was still looking, though. He may have been too busy the past few years for more than fleeting thoughts of those hot summer nights they'd spent together, but he hadn't forgotten. Dew-damp grass. Round July moon. Soft, surrendering sighs. Seeing her again brought all those memories front and center. She'd had an innocence about her back then that had just tangled him up inside, a lack of inhibition that had made him drunk with lust. The taste of her. The sweet, giving heat. *Man, had there been heat.* Enough heat that just seeing her again made him wonder what pretty Peggy was up to these days.

"Cutter—hey, Cutter, over here!"

He whipped his head around, a winning smile in

place as a dozen cameras clicked. He tipped his hat to a little cowboy in tall boots and a big hat who was grinning up at him from the curb as if Cutter held the key to Candyland.

Peg hadn't smiled at him that way. Peg hadn't smiled at all. Her pretty brown eyes had looked right past him while he was still recovering from the punch of pure, spontaneous arousal that had bolted through his body like a summer lightning strike. All flash and fire and electricity.

No. She hadn't smiled. He didn't know quite what to make of that. Everybody smiled for Cutter. Hell. Most women did a lot more than smile. Peg had done a *whole* lot more six years ago. They'd had a good time. At least *he* had. From all indications, she had, too. And now she wouldn't smile for him. He didn't know if that made him feel bad, or mad or just plain puzzled.

Cutter got a line on Peg's straw hat again as she moved easily among the crowd. He caught the smile she gave to a pretty redhead about her age. Scowled as she showed her pearly whites to a gaggle of ranch hands who gaped in awe then panted and groaned in ecstasy as she passed them by.

The booming crack of a cherry bomb sent the bay into a skittering dance that ended up with him snorting and rearing on his hind legs and striking at the air. Cutter settled him with a soft murmur and a strong hand that had the crowd *ahing* in approval just as the band broke into a rousing country rendition of ''God Bless the U.S.A.''

When Cutter looked around, Peg was gone...

without a smile—which, he'd decided, he was going
to get from pretty Peggy before he blew back out of
town tomorrow.

Everybody smiled for Cutter Reno. Everybody.

"Hey, hey, Peggy Sue. I thought that was you, darlin'."

The words—laced with amusement and thick with
pure, male arrogance—drifted across ten yards of
dew-drenched grass and a dome of star-flung sky.
Short of walking straight away and pretending she
hadn't heard him—a long shot since she'd flinched
then frozen like a deer caught in a spotlight the moment she'd heard his voice—Peg had little choice but
to square her shoulders, get ahold of herself and face
him.

She turned slowly, doing her very best not to react
to the picture he made standing there. "Hey, Cutter."

The fireworks had ended less than five minutes ago.
The scent of sulfur from the pyrotechnical display
hung thick on the summer air. Pickups and cars were
still jockeying for exit positions down the narrow
gravel road that led away from Sundown's baseball
park where the fireworks were launched every year.
Shelby, thankfully, was on her way to sleep over with
Peg's folks. She'd been half-asleep in her grandpa
Jack's arms before the last dazzling display had faded
to ash.

The man walking toward her had once held her in
his arms on a starry night much like this one—when
she'd been younger and not as wise and more taken

with a rodeo cowboy's heroic charm than she was today.

He still did make a picture, though, she admitted reluctantly. Lone-wolf rugged and utterly male. That was Cutter. From his tall, broad-shouldered frame, to the sinew and muscle of his athletic swagger, to the dark shadows and shadings of his beautifully sculpted face, to the dark brown hair beneath his black Stetson, he was all male, all sex appeal.

In the starlight, he looked almost hard...until he smiled. Unfortunately, when he smiled, it softened that impossibly virile face, warmed those incredibly blue eyes and reminded her...well, it reminded her of too many things. Like how quick he was to laugh, to tease, to drive her wild with the gentle press or the hot possession of a mouth that had the ability to make her want to forget—even want to forgive—how easy it had been for him to walk away from her.

She settled herself with a deep breath, tucked her fingertips into the hip pockets of the jeans she'd changed into for the night's activities and forced herself to meet his gaze.

"You're lookin' good, darlin'," he said as he walked up to meet her then closed in to stop and stand, boot tip to boot tip, in front of her.

He was crowding her. Not to intimidate. Cutter would never attempt to intimidate even though stacking his six feet against her five and a half, it was a given that he could. No, intimidation wasn't in his nature. Touching was, though. Cutter had always been a toucher and he was about a deep breath away from folding her against him into a long, *hello again* hug.

"You, too, Cutter." She backed what she hoped was a casual step away, refusing to let his compliment, or his use of the word *darlin'*, or his intense, steady appraisal undermine her determination to react to him with a need for anything other than distance. She didn't want to be hugged by Cutter Reno. At least she didn't want to admit that she did.

For the longest moment, he didn't say anything. He just stood there, backlit by moonlight, his expression shadowed by his hat brim. She didn't have to see his face to know that he was trying to figure out her reaction.

"I was surprised to see you back in Sundown, Peg," he said carefully. "Thought that after you finished college, you had your mind set for the city—had plans to be an accountant or something, right?"

He was referring to her long-ago pronouncement of getting an accounting degree then partnering up in some urban firm.

"Yeah, well, you know how it goes. Plans change."

When you're five months pregnant, sick and alone, plans change. It's tough to go to class when you're barfing up your breakfast and your heart is breaking because your baby's not going to have a daddy and the man you were foolish enough to fall in love with has forgotten you even existed.

Since she didn't think he'd particularly want to hear about that and since she had no intention of telling him anyway, she shook off the memory and squared her shoulders.

"Not *your* plans, though," she said in a quick, determined attempt to avert the focus to him. "You did exactly what you said you were going to do. An NFR championship. That's quite an accomplishment."

He shrugged and continued to stare as if he were not only trying to see every detail of her face but right through to every detail of her thoughts, as well. "Guess I've been lucky."

She didn't want to like him for his modesty. It took more than luck to get to the top in the PRCA. It took drive, it took guts and, yeah, it took some luck along with a conviction to not let anything stand in the way. Anything like the woman he'd left behind.

"Well," she said, already deeper into a conversation with him than she'd ever wanted to go, "it was a nice thing you did—coming home to grand marshall the parade and all. Sam was over the moon when you agreed to do it."

He smiled. She quickly looked at her boots while her stomach did a little rock and roll and her heart started that damnable rabbit-run beat again.

"I needed a break—and it's kind of fun being back. Nice to touch base, you know? I hadn't seen Sam or some of the other guys…or you—" he hesitated, his voice going soft and low "—since—well, let's just say it's been a while."

"Yeah." She looked up, briefly meeting his gaze. "It's been a while." Six years is a long while but there was no way she was moving toward that watermark with him.

"So…how's your mom, Cutter? Kind of lost track of her since she moved—what's it been? Almost five years now?"

He slung his weight on one hip, crossed his arms over his chest and tucked his hands under his armpits. "Something like that. She's fine. Likes it in Cheyenne, I guess. Anyway, she did last time I talked to her. I don't see her much, though." He gave a small lift of his shoulders. "You know how it is. I'm on the road a lot."

Yeah. She knew. "Well, that's rodeo."

Silence, as thick as the night, as close as the memories of lying in his arms, mingled with the distant sound of laughter and the occasional explosion of a firecracker. She looked toward the sound. Safe sounds. She had to go. She had to go now.

"Well—"

"—So," he said at the same time, cutting her off. He smiled.

She didn't.

And just when the dead air hanging between them became unbearable, he tilted his head, tried again. "So, what lucky guy coaxed you back to Sundown?" The smile was gone from his voice, an honest curiosity replacing it.

She sniffed, looked past his shoulder toward the city park a few blocks away where Rocky Road, a local country band, was setting up for the dance that would last until midnight.

"Well, let's see, there was a whole raft of them last time I looked."

He chuckled, all soft and low, the sound as intimate as a secret. "I don't doubt it for one little minute. So does that mean you're still footloose and fancy-free?"

About as footloose and fancy-free as a single

mother could be, she thought, biting back the resentment. Not toward Shelby. Shelby was the best thing
that had ever happened to her. The resentment she
felt was reserved for Cutter, for the choices he'd
never been forced to make, the dreams he'd never had
to give up. The resentment was for the fact that his
voice and his smile told her he'd be pleased as punch
to pick up where they'd left off—as long as it was
convenient for him.

You're a jerk, Cutter Reno, she thought but swallowed back the barb. It wouldn't do to blame him—
he was a man, after all, and experience had pretty
much drawn her to the conclusion that it was a condition of the gender. A fair percentage of all men were
jerks. They just couldn't seem to help themselves.

"Well, hey, Cutter," she said with a quick nod and
an obvious intent to call this conversation closed.
"It's been nice talking to you but I've got to go,
okay? Randy's going to be wondering where I am."
She shouldered past him. "Good to see you."

"Hey, wait." He snagged her arm, spun her back
toward him with a good-natured laugh. "Randy? As
in, Randy *Bubba* Watkins?" His eyes were crinkled
at the corners, no doubt picturing bowlegged, buck-
toothed Bubba whose name was the first one that had
popped into Peg's head. "You and Bubba? You've
got a thing goin'?"

Clearly he wasn't buying it. Which, of course, he
was right not to since she and Randy had never been
and would never be anything but friends.

"Why not Randy?" She lifted her chin, relying on
the premise that the best defense was just that—de-

fense—all the while carefully removing his hand from around her upper arm and working to tamp down the sizzle of heat his touch had sent skittering along her skin. "He's one of the good guys. He's funny. He's kind. And he sticks, you know what I mean?"

The minute her last statement popped out, and sounding way too accusatory, she realized her error. Just as she realized that Cutter understood her point and recognized her anger. He'd neither stuck around nor kept in touch once he'd left her and Sundown behind all those years ago.

He thumbed back his hat; his dark brows lowered over ridiculously thick-lashed eyes. She could see he was warming up to be charitable and that sat just about as well as his arrogance.

"Peg—about that summer—"

"—I wish I could stay and talk, I really do." She cut him off before he made her so mad she'd do something unforgivable, like show him just how much his presence back in Sundown had shaken her. "But I've got to go."

She set out again, walking in long, purposeful strides across the outfield. "You take care now," she added over her shoulder just to make sure he understood that he hadn't rattled her.

Because he had rattled her—and rattled her good—she broke into a fast jog when she had the good luck to spot Randy, who was as surprised as he was pleased when she snagged his hand. Wrapping her arm around his waist, she started chattering cheerfully about the band and the dance he had promised her. And she told herself she wasn't running, that Cutter didn't have the power to make her run. Not toward him. Not away.

Alone, in the dark, Cutter watched and wondered and tried to decide exactly how disappointed he was that Peg had just thrown him the coldest shoulder between here and Bozeman.

Lucky man, he thought about Bubba as he walked toward his truck debating whether or not his night was over or just beginning. Some warm-up drumbeats and a few licks from a bass guitar rumbled across the night from the park.

He thought about his empty room in Sundown's historic old hotel. He thought of pretty Peggy who would be at the dance—with Bubba.

Then he thought, "What the hell."

He fished his keys out of his front jeans pocket and swung up into the cab. As he turned the ignition, he grinned as the words to an old country song came to mind. "If Bubba can dance, I can, too."

Two

"Alley cat," Peg sputtered on her way home from work the next day.

She didn't want to but she couldn't stop thinking about Cutter and the way he'd posed and prowled and strutted his stuff for all the panting little buckle bunnies who had drooled over him at the dance last night.

"Yep. Alley cat tags him in a nutshell," she decided as she turned down the street that led to Krystal's who, in addition to being her best friend, also baby-sat for Shelby while Peg worked at Lathrop's Feed Store where she kept books for her dad.

Too bad she hadn't been able to figure Cutter out six years ago. At eighteen his smiles had said, "You're special." At eighteen, she'd been in love. After all, he'd been daring. A rodeo cowboy. A mysterious breed. A local boy who had returned victorious. And he'd been so beautiful it had made her chest ache.

She let out a deep breath, pressed a closed fist to a spot between her breasts and told herself it wasn't aching now because of him. Now that he was back—victorious again. And even more beautiful.

Face grim, Peg pulled to a stop in front of Krystal's house and killed the engine. Well, he may be back, but this time, there would be no repeat performance of that summer.

She'd been so stupid. The rodeo had been in town for an eight-day run for the Fourth of July holiday then, too. Since she'd had a crush on Cutter when he'd been a senior in high school and she'd been a sophomore, she'd been pretty much a sure thing. He'd known it. He'd played on it. It had taken him five days to talk her out of her virginity.

He'd been good, she remembered as she slipped out of her beat-up old truck then walked up Krystal's front walk that was bordered with valiantly blooming summer flowers. So good. Sweet and attentive. Intense and enduring. He'd taught her about sex. He'd taught her about love. And then he'd taught her about heartache.

He'd left with a promise to call from Salt Lake. She hadn't heard from him or seen him since.

Until yesterday.

"His loss," she breathed on a wind-down sigh as she strolled through the front door and scooped her beautiful little five-year-old tomboy into her arms.

"Him who, Momma?" Shelby asked after a big hug and a squirming wiggle.

"Nobody, cupcake. Nobody."

"Any *nobody* I know?"

Peg met Krystal's bright eyes with a glare meant to silence.

Krystal either wasn't paying attention or chose to ignore the warning. "You can fool some of the people all of th—"

"—Just stop. I'm not trying to fool anybody," she insisted as Shelby slid out of her arms.

Krystal made sure Shelby was back on her tummy on the floor and engrossed in her coloring book. "So that means you were planning on telling me you talked to Cutter last night?" she asked softly.

Peg lifted a shoulder, a failed attempt at indifference. She'd known that someone would have seen them talking just as she'd known the word would get around. Newsworthy or not, the word always got around in Sundown. "So I saw him. So what."

"So—how'd it go?"

Peg crossed to the island counter nestled in the middle of Krystal's cheery yellow kitchen, gave Grant a grinning hello then dug into the perpetually stocked cookie jar. She bit into a crunchy peanut-butter cookie, closed her eyes on a hum of approval and swallowed.

"It didn't *go* anywhere." She touched a finger to the corner of her mouth to catch a crumb and tuck it into her mouth. "We ran into each other after the fireworks. No big deal."

"Big deal," Krystal pointed out unnecessarily. "What did you two talk about?"

Another shrug. "I told him I was involved with someone."

Krystal blinked. "Really? Well, now. That's a pretty tough trick since all you do is work and, oh, yeah...*work*," she added with feeling as she moved to snag a crayon from Grant's pudgy little fist before he ate it. "So who's the lucky guy?"

Peg grinned guiltily. "Randy?"

Krystal let out a hoot of laughter as she wiped Grant's fingers with a towel and handed him a cookie. "So Randy must be, like, on cloud nine, huh?"

"Randy's a pal. And he doesn't know that we have this hot and heavy thing going."

"Must be a lot of fun for him."

Peg sank down on a kitchen chair. "Look. Cutter will be gone soon—if he isn't already—and then we can just forget this whole thing."

"What thing, Momma?" Shelby asked from the floor where she was sprawled on her tummy finishing her masterpiece with crayon and coloring paper.

Peg scowled at Krystal before turning a smile to her daughter. "It's a girl thing, Shell. A *big* girl thing. Hey, is that for me?" she asked, her voice full of hope for Shelby's benefit as she looked at the picture of a cowboy riding a big black horse. Her darling girl had worked so hard to keep the colors between the lines.

"For Grandpa."

"He's going to love it. Next one's mine, though, okay?"

"I'll make another real pretty one."

"Outside," Krystal mouthed over Shelby's head and swung Grant onto her hip.

Peg rolled her eyes, snagged another cookie and reluctantly followed Krystal out onto the backyard deck. She wasn't up for this lecture but it looked like it was going to happen anyway.

The next day was Peg's Thursday off. She planned to spend it like she always did. With Shelby still asleep, she dressed in her chore clothes, figuring on passing the hour between seven and eight mucking out stalls and telling the horses how pretty they were. When Shelby got up, they'd have breakfast then go for their Thursday morning ride.

Carrying her boots, she slipped quietly out the kitchen door and headed down to her little barn. The morning was already July warm, the sun a burning fireball suspended in the stunning blue Montana sky. The air was rich with summer scents: drying grass, ripening hay and the fragrance of wildflowers drifting down from the high meadows.

Nestled against the breath-stealing backdrop of the mountains, her little place didn't look like much. Actually it wasn't even hers, though she thought of it that way. For the time being, she had to be content to rent the house and the three acres that sat on the edge of town from Homer Carmichael. Until she finally wore him down and convinced him to sell it to her, it was the best she could do. When Homer was ready, though, she would be, too. She could afford a contract—if the down payment wasn't too steep—and if that old truck kept running, she thought with a frown and tugged on her boots.

In the meantime, the rent Homer charged was fair; it met her budget and he didn't care what she did to the place in the way of making it her own. Hers and Shelby's.

Rascal, their four-year-old black-and-white border collie, lay in a slant of morning sunlight that filtered in through the open barn door. Dreaming of chasing rabbits, she thought with a smile as his feet fluttered and his tail thumped in his sleep.

Grabbing a grain scoop, she filled a feed bucket with the special blend Jack had mixed up for her. She'd been thinking about her father a lot the last couple of days—not Jack, but her biological father, a man she'd never known. Jack Lathrop was her dad in every way that counted, in every way but blood. She loved him and all the memories of his loving hands and gentle smiles that he'd given her so generously from the time she could remember. And yet, sometimes, she wondered. What was he like? Where was he now?

Thoughtful, she filled Henry's then Bea's feed trough, gave them each an affectionate pat on the rump and dipped the scoop back in the bucket.

"And how are you, you ornery outlaw?" she murmured when Jackpot, the three-year-old gelding she'd brought home just this past month, nickered and pumped his head. "Trying to decide if you want to take a bite out of me or dig into your chow, aren't ya, big guy?" she crooned, filling his trough as well.

Her weakness for a pretty face had gotten her in

trouble again with this guy. Jackpot was a hot-blooded black-and-white paint that her friends, Lee and Ellie Savage, had insisted she accept for her birthday gift last month. Even knowing that the Savage's sole income didn't come from their breeding business, Jackpot was still an extravagant gift.

"I can't," Peg had sputtered, flabbergasted.

"Yes," Lee had said with a grin the day Ellie had invited Peg out to Shiloh Ranch to visit, "you can. I don't have time to mess with him," Lee had added. "But you—with a little TLC and a gentle hand—you just might reform him."

Well. There it was. She'd always been a sucker for an outlaw and now she had one of her very own.

Another outlaw had her thinking about her father again. Cutter showing up back in Sundown had dredged up all kinds of thoughts, all kinds of questions, and resurrected the what-ifs she rarely let herself dwell on. What if she'd known her real father? Would she be different? Would her life be different?

And what about Shelby? What if Shelby knew about Cutter? What if Cutter knew about Shelby?

Scowling, she tossed the grain bucket and scoop back in the bin. She couldn't honestly think that she'd done the wrong thing by keeping it from him all these years, even though Krystal—who was the only person besides her mother and Jack who knew that Cutter was Shelby's father—had lectured her good and long yesterday afternoon about the possibility that it was.

"He has a right, Peg. He has a right to know," Krystal had insisted gently.

Peg hadn't felt one bit gentle. "He has no rights.

Not with Shelby. He lost any right when he left without so much as a long look back. Promise me. Promise me that you and Sam didn't tell him anything about Shelby.''

Of course Krystal had promised. They hadn't told, even though Cutter had fired questions at them like bullets at the picnic, wanting to know all about what she'd been up to. Peg wouldn't let herself—not for a minute—feel wrong about not telling him. Just as it didn't feel wrong that she thought of Jack as her dad.

Snagging the knife she kept tucked on a beam over the tack room door, she cut the twine on a hay bale. Like Cutter, her own biological father had been a rodeo rider. She hadn't even known he existed until she'd come home from college, pregnant and ashamed and needing her mother.

With her arms warm and forgiving around her, Kay Lathrop had told Peg about her blood father then. It had been a gift. An acknowledgment that people made mistakes. That Kay had made one, too, and that her world hadn't ended. In fact, Jack had married her, adopted Peg and they had been her world. Her whole world. Just like Shelby was Peg's.

As she tossed a fat flake of hay into each manger, she thought about the choices she'd made. Tough choices. Now, more than ever, after seeing Cutter again, watching the way he'd flirted and flitted from one woman to another at the dance, knowing the way he lived, chasing the next gold buckle, following the circuit, she was convinced she'd made the right ones. Cutter wasn't daddy or husband material.

Did she feel guilty that she hadn't given him a

chance to be either? Sometimes, she admitted, as she unrolled the water hose, lifted the catch on the faucet and started filling the tanks with fresh water. But guilt didn't override one unalterable fact. She and Shelby were here. And Cutter was long gone. Again. At least, by her calculations, he should have left yesterday. After all, there was nothing keeping him in Sundown and a lot to lead him away. His type always had a reason to ride off into the sunset.

She ignored the little pang of longing that always tagged along behind any thought associated with him as she shut off the water then maneuvered the wheelbarrow over behind the stalls. She picked up the pitchfork, balanced it over the handles of the wheelbarrow. Some things just weren't meant to be.

And that was fine. *She* was fine. The unexpected bite of tears that stung her eyes wasn't anything more than a temporary, knee-jerk yearning for what never could have been.

She sniffed them back, swiped at her eyes with the back of a gloved hand and shook it off. There. Better already.

Forcefully shifting her thoughts from stolen kisses and lean, strong heat to her mom's recipe for blueberry pancakes, she tried to remember whether or not she had the makings in her cupboard. Shelby Lynn dearly loved blueberry pancakes. And it was Shelby Lynn that she had to take care of today and every day.

Cutter was still trying to figure out why he'd just driven into a lane with a mailbox that told him

P. Lathrop lived in the little two-story clapboard house with the sagging front porch and sun-faded gray siding. With his pickup engine idling softly, he sat behind the wheel and couldn't come up with a particularly good answer.

"You should leave it be, Reno," he muttered, as a black-and-white border collie came lumbering up to his truck, tongue lolling and tail wagging.

What point did he plan to make? What good was he up to? Honest truth? None. He should just go. Yet he killed the motor and climbed out of the truck, stretching out the kinks that were his rewards for his fair share of failed eight counts and board-hard motel beds.

He patted the dog's head then followed him to the barn where the doors were open and a bluesy country tune played softly from a radio that was standard equipment in any horse barn he'd ever encountered.

His boot heels crunched through Montana dust until he stopped just inside the wide double-door frame. As his eyes adjusted to the dim interior light, his blood started a slow, mellow simmer at the sight that greeted him there.

No way should she make his blood heat, let alone boil. Not turned out like that. The punch of arousal was hard and strong. So was the kick of reality. He realized with one look how much he still wanted her—and how hard she had it on her own as she worked at mucking out a stall.

He drew another deep breath, knowing he should just turn around and go...but all he could do was stand and stare as she stood in a slant of sunlight.

On her feet were knee-high rubber muck boots. Her shirt—a dust-gray tank top—left her tanned arms bare and those beautiful breasts lost somewhere beneath the sloppy cotton knit. Hanging from her hips was a pair of baggy silk boxer shorts that might have once been siren-red but had faded with many washings and wearings to an anemic pink. The bare, tanned line of leg exposed between boot and shorts was long and coltishly lean. Beneath those ridiculously ugly shorts, her hips were slim, her buttocks tight and high and he could just make out the faint outline of French-cut panties.

He couldn't help but wonder if she was wearing lace under all that utilitarian clothing as his gaze drifted to her hair. She'd tied it up high at the back of her head into a sweeping ponytail that made her look about sixteen years old instead of the twenty-four that he knew her to be. A pretty little scrap of red ribbon held it precariously in place.

That one small concession to her femininity did things to his heart rate he didn't even want to think about and made him realize he had no business poking his nose—or anything else—into Peg Lathrop's homespun little world. She was as off-limits to a guy like him as a nine-to-five job and roots. In some ways, he'd known it six years ago. Well, after seeing her like this, he definitely knew it now. This was a home-and-hearth kind of girl. This was a woman who deserved a lot more than the one-night stand that he grudgingly admitted he might have come out here hoping to charm out of her—for old times' sake. For sentimentality sake.

Hell, for his sake.

He should go. For her sake.

But then she turned around and spotted him—and he'd be damned if he could find a convincing reason to go anywhere.

"Helluva watchdog you've got here, darlin'." He leaned a shoulder against the doorjamb and shoved his hands into his hip pockets. Then he tried to act like his knees didn't feel like putty and his heart wasn't goading him to walk right on over there and kiss her until they fell to the barn floor in a tangled knot of hot, hungry hands and arching bodies.

He wasn't the only one who'd been caught off guard. Those big cinnamon-brown eyes of hers had grown wide before they'd narrowed in what he was pretty sure was anger, not welcome. He didn't want Peg angry with him, which, if he were being totally honest, was another reason he was still in Sundown.

She'd talked a good talk the other night when he'd caught up with her after the fireworks. She'd played it real cool. But there had been a spark of anger in her eyes when she'd faced him and for that, he'd felt guilty. And then at the dance, she'd made damn sure he didn't get within a Texas-two-step of her. Not that he would have poached on Randy's territory, but it hadn't taken long to figure out she'd just been using Randy as a smoke screen. That friendship was the only thing going on between those two, had been obvious from the get-go.

He hadn't pushed it, though, even though he'd wanted to. Yeah, he'd wanted a chance to hold her close in a slow, sultry dance in the moonlight. A chance to feel all that soft, woman heat molded against him. But he'd had no chance. Not with her. Not last night.

He supposed that was another reason why he was here today. Just like he supposed he knew why she wasn't happy with him. He'd told her he loved her that long ago summer and, well, the fact was he had. Hell, he'd fallen a little in love with every pretty girl he'd ever been with. Just not enough to stay.

Peg…Peg had been special, though. Maybe because he'd been her first. Maybe because she'd loved so freely. It had been hard to leave her. But he'd left anyway. Yeah, he'd left her with a shiny gold buckle that he'd won in the rodeo and a promise to call her— which, he was pretty sure, he'd never done.

Until he'd seen her the other night under the stars, he'd never felt near bad enough about running out on her like that. But *she* had. Her eyes had said that she'd felt real bad. And he guessed maybe that was another one of the reasons he'd shown up here today. He still hadn't seen her smile. The way things were stacking up, he had a feeling he wasn't going to anytime soon, either.

"Thought you'd left," she said, turning back to her wheelbarrow and filling another pitchfork full of the stuff that a rodeo cowboy considered beneath him to even think about let alone clean out of a stall.

"Well, I was going to, Peg. I truly was, but then I got to thinkin'."

She tossed a glare over her shoulder that had him scratching his head and grinning.

"Yeah. I know. Imagine that. Me—having a thought."

When she didn't return his smile but turned back to her work instead, he walked into the barn, picked out a stall post that afforded him the best view and leaned against it.

"See, the thing is, what I was thinkin' was that we had a real good thing going that summer, Peg."

She stiffened, straightened, squared her shoulders. When she met his gaze this time, the fire in her eyes could have lit a blowtorch. "And you thought it might be a fine idea if we sort of picked up where we left off before you hit the road again?"

Bull's-eye. He shoved away from the post, grabbed the fork out of her hands—damned if he knew why— and took over her job. "Actually I was remembering how pretty your smile was. And I was thinkin' I was sorry if I was the one who stole it."

He watched her face over a pitchfork full of soiled straw and about three feet of dead silence.

The fire dimmed and she finally smiled, but it wasn't the one he remembered. This smile was brittle and bitter and way too cynical for those petal-soft lips that had once touched his with hunger and need.

"Don't flatter yourself, Cutter. You may fancy yourself a heartbreaker but I promise you, you left mine in one very solid piece."

Well, he didn't know what to think about that. A part of him had kind of hoped he *had* broken her heart—maybe just a little. Just enough to miss him. After all, she'd said she loved him, too.

He scowled, puzzled. So this was how the shoe felt

on the other foot. He couldn't say he much liked the fit. Just like his ego wasn't quite ready to buy her denial. Maybe it was a pride thing. It wasn't easy to think that he'd meant so little to her—whoa—like maybe *his* walking away had told her that *she* had meant so little to him.

It was years too late, but in that moment, he finally understood that her pride came into play here, too.

"Go away, Cutter," she said, trying to reclaim the fork. "I've got work to do—and I'm sure you've got a bronc or a buckle bunny to ride somewhere."

He couldn't even be offended. She pretty much had him tagged, but he held on and there they stood, her glaring and him grinning and totally without a clue how all his good intentions had turned into this little pissing contest over a forkful of smelly horse manure.

"As a matter of fact," he said, warming to the challenge in her eyes and the expanding memory that Peg Lathrop had been as wild a ride as any bronc he'd ever drawn and more fun than a goat rope, "I seem to find myself with a couple of days on my hands."

Well, hell. Where had that come from? He didn't have any free time. He was due to ride somewhere— couldn't think where at the moment—but he knew he was due somewhere tomorrow night.

"I'm happy for you," she said between clenched teeth. "So go do something productive with your time. Learn a skill."

That finally made him laugh. "Damn, I've missed that mouth."

"Yeah, right. That's why you came racing back here after, gosh, only six years."

"I knew it," he said, unable to keep the gloat from his voice. "You're mad as hell. That means you missed me."

"Like a toothache. Now, give me the damn pitchfork."

He held tight when she tugged. "Promise not to use it on me?"

"Unlike some people, I never make promises I don't intend to keep."

He winced. "Ouch. Guess I deserved that."

"And I deserve to be able to eat all the chocolate I want and not have it go to my hips. It's a cruel world."

"Come on, Peg. I'm trying to apolo—"

"Mommy? Mommy, I'm hungry."

Cutter blinked, stopped midapology and whipped his head around to the sound. Then all he could do was stare at a little blond moppet dressed in a soft pink, knee-length nightie, a pair of scruffy red cowboy boots and a head full of baby-fine bed hair.

Mommy?

He was still recovering from that little shock when he turned back to Peg. Her eyes rounded with distress, then darkened with warning just before she let go of the fork and made a beeline for the little girl.

"Hey, baby." Her voice turned as soft as butter. In long, determined strides, she walked to her daughter—*her daughter*—turned her around by her shoulders and herded her back toward the house. "I'm all finished here. How about some pancakes?"

"Blueberry?"

"You bet."

The little girl peeked back around behind her then up at her mother. "Who's that man?"

"He was just asking for directions and now he's moving on." She glared over her shoulder as she said it in a flat-out invitation to leave.

"Did you tell him how to get where he's s'posed to go?" the little girl asked as she walked ahead of her mother.

"Well, I sure tried, honey," Peg said, her voice trailing behind her. "I sure did try to tell him where to go."

Cutter heard every word of the conversation. Some of it even registered—especially the telling him where to go part. But over it all, hung the presence of that little blond-haired girl.

Peg had a child.

Talk about a new wrinkle. She had a little girl. A little girl in a pink nightie and cowboy boots. Red cowboy boots. The picture made him grin—but it faded as his curiosity grew—right along with a little prickle of something that felt suspiciously like irritation.

Well, it wasn't like he'd expected her to pine for him. He rolled a shoulder. Not forever, at any rate.

But a child.

Wreck Grover, a bronc rider from Butte that he partnered up with sometimes, had a little girl. Katie must be about five years old now. Looked to be about the same size as Peg's little one. He stroked a hand over his jaw. *Didn't waste much time forgetting about you, did she, Reno?*

Something about that just didn't set right. Something about it had him watching where they'd walked long after they'd climbed the porch steps and the door had closed behind them. And something made him feel a little uneasy and for some unknown reason, excluded.

Peg was a momma. And last night, she'd let him know that she wasn't attached. The notion of some good-for-nothing smooth-talker laying his hands on her, getting her pregnant then leaving her to fend for herself made him mad as hell.

And he was making a lot of assumptions. Maybe it didn't shake down that way at all. Maybe she'd been married. Maybe they were divorced. Maybe he died.

He cupped his nape then tipped his black Resistol lower on his forehead. And maybe he shouldn't be standing here speculating when it was really none of his business. He'd only driven out here to see if he could get that smile out of her—and maybe a little lovin' for old times' sake. It wasn't like he wanted to make a commitment or anything. Ha. Wouldn't that be a joke?

So why wasn't he laughing?

Slowly, with his fingertips tucked in his back pockets, he walked back out into the sun. The border collie trotted out to greet him, nudging his muzzle against Cutter's leg, begging for a quick pat as he passed him by, heading for the truck. He'd just opened the driver's-side door and was about to hike himself up and in, when he noticed movement on the front porch.

Peg's little girl had slipped back outside. She was standing snug against a porch post, half-hidden, obviously shy as she peeked around the post, her big eyes watchful, her smile tentative and unsure.

He should just drive away.

"How's it goin' today, little blondie?" he asked, instead, one foot on the running board, the other still planted on the ground.

Her giggle was like a bright, shiny penny. "I'm not blondie. I'm Shelby."

"Shelby. Well, now, that's a mighty pretty name for a mighty pretty girl. You're pretty like your momma, did you know that?"

"Yup," she said with the unabashed honesty of a child who was well loved and had his grin stretching wider.

She raised a tiny hand and brushed a swatch of hair back from her face. "You were in the parade. I saw you."

"Did you, now?"

She nodded and dressed in her nightie and bed hair and red boots, came scooting down the steps. "Are you really a sheriff?"

He grinned through a puzzled frown then finally figured out what she was talking about. "Marshall, darlin'. Not sheriff. I was the grand *marshall* of the parade. Nobody in their right mind would ever give me a real badge."

"Why?" she asked, all big round eyes and crumbling smile. "Are you a bad guy?"

He looked at this little girl, at the blue eyes that he'd been trying not to notice and whose bold sweetness tugged at him in a way no child had ever tugged at him before. He thought about her mother who wasn't just mad at him—she didn't much like him, either.

And he'd be damned if he knew how to answer her.

Three

———

"Stupid. Stupid. Stupid," Peg sputtered under her breath as she washed her hands then banged around in the cupboards for the griddle and a mixing bowl. She'd been sniping at Cutter over a pitchfork for pity sake.

"Why didn't you just take out an ad? Cutter Reno Punches All My Hot Buttons."

She braced her palms on the counter, drew a deep breath. Tried to steady herself. And got mad all over again. Darn it. He *did* punch her buttons, but if she was angry with anyone, it ought to be with herself.

Okay. So he'd caught her off guard. He'd been the last—the *very* last—person she'd expected to see today. Why wasn't he gone from Sundown? Why had he come sniffing around out here? And why did her heart skip and stutter and generally send her blood into sizzle mode every time she encountered his handsome, renegade face?

"Because you haven't learned a thing in six years, that's why," she admitted grumpily. Snagging a carton of milk and an egg from the fridge, she added them to the flour mix she'd dumped into the bowl. "And because you panicked."

She whipped a spoon through the pancake mix, blew a stray fall of hair away from her face. She'd panicked because he was still in Sundown kicking up her heartbeat—panicked at the look in his eyes when Shelby had come pattering out to the barn.

Her stomach sank just thinking about it. A thin layer of perspiration broke out across her brow, beaded at the small of her back. Shelby. He'd seen Shelby.

And she'd overreacted. She'd let him see—oh, Lord, had she let him see how desperate she'd been to get Shelby out of his sight? Cutter may be selfish and self-centered, but he wasn't stupid. And the look on his face—had it just been surprise? Or had it been recognition? Had he seen his eyes in the eyes of her daughter? Her daughter who sometimes asked about her daddy?

It's kind of like your friend, Kelly. Some kids just don't have daddies.

But Kelly does have a daddy. He just went away. Did my daddy go away, too?

What do you say to your child who doesn't understand the reason but feels the loss? How do you explain why Grant has a daddy who tucks him in at night and shares a bed with his mommy?

You have Grampa Jack, Shell. Grampa Jack loves you as much as any daddy could. And Gramma Kay loves you. And Krystal and Grant and Sam. And our friends Lee and Ellie? They all love you. But nobody loves you as much as I do, okay?

And nobody did love Shelby as much as she did. Nobody could. It wouldn't be long before her evasive answers wouldn't be enough for her daughter, though. And what would she tell her then?

And why, just because Cutter was in the neighborhood, did she feel a guilt that was neither warranted nor wise? Telling him would come to no good for anyone. She'd always known that. It was just like she'd told Krystal yesterday.

"What do you think would happen if I told him, Kris? He'd just feel guilty and beholden—probably even make a token effort to play the part. But in the long run, he'd leave. Cowboys make an art out of leaving. And Shelby, who loves cowboys, would be left with a broken heart when her cowboy daddy lit out because riding wild horses is more important to him than his child."

Or his child's mother, she thought grimly, as she opened the freezer door, rummaged around and found a package of blueberries she'd frozen last summer. She stuck them in the microwave, punched the touch pads and waited for them to defrost. Hands planted on her hips, she scowled at the revolving glass dish through the windowed door, not liking the part of her that sometimes played with the idea of telling him anyway—just to see him sweat. Just to see him squirm. Just to see him go pale and apologetic and realize that he'd missed his chance with her and with their beautiful daughter.

No. He'd missed his chance with *her* daughter. Shelby was hers, only hers and she wouldn't risk Shelby's precious little heart just to indulge in a little vindictive retribution. She would never put Shelby at risk that way—she'd told Krystal that, too.

"I did him a favor, and you know it. And if I'd told him, you and I both know the only satisfaction *I'd* get is revenge. Admittedly it sounds sweet sometimes, but it's not my style. If it had been, I'd have let Jack drag Cutter back to Sundown six years ago and tie him to a life that would have made him miserable. Then Shelby would have suffered in the process, too."

And she would have suffered, as well, but she hadn't confessed that to Krystal. The look in her friend's eyes had said she didn't have to.

The microwave beeped several times before she had the presence of mind to snap out of her little trance and retrieve the blueberries.

Well, it was all a moot point now anyway. They'd seen the last of Cutter Reno. He should be well on his way out of Sundown by now—which reminded her. Shelby should have washed up and changed by now, too.

"Shelby Lynn," she called over her shoulder as she drained the berries in a colander then started folding them carefully into the batter. "Come on, baby, I'm just about ready to start cookin'. I need you to set the table."

She'd expected to hear Shelby tripping down the

stairs as she hurried to the kitchen, always excited by the prospect of helping out. Instead she heard the front door open then close and then the sound of Shelby's footsteps echoing on the hard wood foyer floor. Mixed with the mini clomp of Shelby's little boots was the faint click of Rascal's paws—and the unmistakable ring of heavier footsteps.

She froze—then spun around so quickly she almost dropped the bowl of pancake batter. She nearly dropped it anyway when she saw what Shelby had in tow.

"This cowboy's hungry, Mom," Shelby said brightly, having clearly decided that the only thing to do about it was feed him.

Cutter, holding his hat in one hand and her daughter's hand in the other, grinned sheepishly from the kitchen door.

"I hope I'm not intruding."

Like hell, she thought and spun back to the counter before she said something she'd be way too sorry for.

Cutter sat at Peg's table looking around the small but homey kitchen with its light blue walls and dark blue curtains. He listened with half an ear to Shelby chatter about Bea, her POA, as she explained proudly but unnecessarily that POA stood for Pony of America—a breed evolved from a cross between a pony and an appaloosa horse. Then she moved on to her favorite TV shows and anything else that popped into her active little mind. All the while, she alternately ate and sneaked bites of her pancake to the border collie who knew he'd hit the gravy train and lay patiently beneath the table.

Well, he thought, as he risked a glance at Peg over his plate, at least *one* of the Lathrop girls was hospitable.

Oh, Peg was trying. Trying hard to be polite. Trying hard to smile at his little jokes. Trying hard to act as if she wouldn't find extreme pleasure seeing him staked bare-ass naked over a bed of cactus under a red-hot sun after a gallon of saltwater had been poured down his throat.

"More pancakes, Cutter?" she asked, all sweetness and light through a strained but determined smile.

"Why, sure thing, Peg. Been a while since I've had any home cookin'. A man would be a fool to turn down any kind of an offer from a pretty woman—especially one who cooks like you do."

Just like a man would be a fool to keep goading her that way. There was fire behind that benign smile. Flames shooting from those spicy-brown eyes. She'd clearly understood that the "cookin'" he'd had in mind had nothing to do with kitchens and everything to do with what they'd once done in the dark with their clothes off.

A man who didn't understand women as well as he did might get to thinking that he wasn't welcome here. But if there was anything Cutter understood, it was broncs and women. And he understood that little Peg still cared about him. She didn't want to. Just like she didn't want to be mad—and there was the rub. If she didn't care, then she wouldn't *be* mad. Both prospects had him wondering and wanting to get just a little better feel for exactly what it was going to take to land in her good graces again.

It didn't make sense that he cared, really. She had her life—that cute little blonde was proof of that—and he had his. It wasn't as if he had the time or the inclination to stick around. Yet here he sat—in the middle of her sunny kitchen, with little green plants sitting on the windowsill over the sink and finger-paint masterpieces papering her ancient refrigerator door. Yep, here he sat, liking what he was seeing and getting fuzzy little pictures of what it would be like to have the right to sit at this table as more than an unwelcome guest.

"Mom and me are goin' ridin' right after breakfast, right, Mom? You should go with us, Cutter," he heard Shelby state as if it were a foregone conclusion just as Peg dropped another pancake on his plate.

He looked up, not into Shelby's eyes but into the eyes of her momma who, he could see by her pointed look, had a real definite opinion of what his response to Shelby's invitation should be.

It was pure orneriness—he couldn't seem to help himself—that had him turning his grin on Shelby as he poured warm maple syrup over his pancake. "Why sure, darlin', if you want me to."

"Shelby, Cutter's a busy man," Peg put in as she turned back to her griddle. She shut off the flame on the burner, but his temperature rose a couple of notches at the sight of what he'd be willing to wager was the sweetest little backside east or west of the Rockies. She'd ditched her work boots and was stand-ing barefoot in the kitchen. There was something powerfully sexy about a barefoot woman—and those baggy silk shorts and that sloppy gray tank top were going to be his undoing yet.

"He doesn't have time to go riding this morning," he heard her add over the haze of sexual heat.

"But he just said he could go."

"He was just being polite, weren't you, Cutter?"

Cutter leaned back in his chair, tilted his head and smiled into eyes that had turned as cold as frost in a Montana winter. "Actually I'm free as a bird."

"See?" Shelby insisted.

"Honey, we don't really have anything for him to ride."

"Jackpot," Shelby said and Cutter could almost hear the "duh."

Peg cleared her throat. "Sweetie, Jackpot's barely green broke. He's not ready to ride yet, you know that."

"But Cutter's a cowboy. He rides wild horses," Shelby insisted. "Don't ya, Cutter?"

Cutter propped his elbow on the table, his chin in his hand and grinned. "Well, I surely have been known to."

"And he can use your old saddle. It used to be Grampa Jack's, didn't it, Mom? But Grampa got me and Mom new saddles for Christmas so now we got an extra one."

A long second passed before Peg's expression transformed from one of backed-into-a-corner acceptance to a you-asked-for-it-you-got-it smile.

"Fine," she said stiffly. "You want to ride a wild horse, you've got one. Just don't say I didn't warn you. Oh, and when we ride, we ride for a couple of hours. I *surely* hope you're up for more than your usual eight seconds.''

Cutter chuckled, low and easy. "Why, yes, ma'am. I reckon I've got more than eight seconds in me. But then, I guess you already know that, don't you?"

The ice in her gaze melted to fire again in a heartbeat. He felt the burn clear across the table.

"I'll do up the dishes, Shell," she said stiffly. "You go on up and get dressed. Bring your brush down with you, sweetie, and I'll fix your hair."

"Okay!" Shelby shot out of the chair and raced toward the stairs. "Come on, Rascal." The dog trotted after her like a shadow.

"Let me help you with those," Cutter offered— and rather magnanimously, he thought—as he stacked his fork and knife on his plate.

"Sit," Peg snapped and rounded on him. "You just sit right where you are."

She grabbed his plate, then pointed a fork at him. "Don't you come into my house," she warned him as brilliant color flooded her cheeks and her breath came hard and fast, "and in front of my daughter...start making your sly sexual innuendoes and... and..."

He snagged her wrist in one hand, relieved her of the plate and fork with his other and set them back on the table. "And look at you like I want to kiss you?"

With his hand still clamped around her wrist, he stood, walked around the table until he was directly in front of her. And suddenly he did want to kiss her—much more than he wanted to tease her.

She was backing a slow foot away to every step he took toward her until she'd backed as far as she could go. Her hips connected with the counter about the same time as his hips connected with hers. She was shaking her head, but her eyes...her eyes weren't in agreement. And it was her eyes that he chose to believe.

"So, what do you say, Peg? Can I kiss you? Just once? Just to see if it's as good as I remember?"

She wasn't looking at him now. She was looking anywhere but at him. Her pretty cheeks were flaming red. Her eyes were a little wild with panic and denial and a desire that he recognized even if she didn't.

"Just once," he murmured, easing up closer against her, fitting the length of him against the length of her, savoring the contact of lush breasts, long legs.

He released her wrist and because he couldn't stop himself, tangled his fingers in her hair—in the long, silky length of it—and tugged the ribbon free. He'd been wanting to do that, too, ever since he'd seen her in the sunlight in the barn.

Her hair fell into his hands like a waterfall of silk. He gathered it up, brought it to his face, inhaled the Montana morning scent of it, the lustrous weight and the soft womanly fragrance.

"Don't," she whispered, but with little force behind the word, as he tunneled his fingers up to the base of her scalp to cup and caress her head, to tip her face up to his with a gentle pressure of his thumbs beneath her jaw.

"It's okay," he murmured, barely touching his mouth to hers, drowning in the feel of her, the shimmering warmth of her breath quivering against his lips. "It's just a kiss."

He brushed his mouth over hers, softly seeking, gently teasing until seeking and teasing weren't nearly enough.

"Just a kiss," he repeated, opened his mouth firmly over hers—and got hopelessly, unalterably lost.

Sweet heaven. It was just her mouth. Just her warm, wet, wonderfully erotic mouth—and he wanted it. He wanted it open for his tongue. Wanted her willingly inviting him inside. And when, at last, she did, he claimed it as his, wouldn't let her close it to him. Not yet. Not for another million years if he could arrange it.

With his hands bracketing her jaw, he indulged in her, remembered how much he'd missed her, how quickly she could fire him up this way. Good Lord, what she did to him. Even her resistance was sweet as she pressed her hands against his chest and pushed, then knotted them into fists that grasped his shirt and dragged him closer, invited him deeper.

"Sweet, sweet Peggy," he murmured, breaking away long enough to change the angle, heighten the contact as he wedged a leg between her thighs. Sliding his hands down her body, he filled his palms with the delectable curve of her bottom and her mouth with the ebb and flow of his tongue.

She tasted like maple syrup and blueberries and woman. Like hunger and anticipation and the sensual edge of desire. Memories of the girl who had given herself to him so freely joined forces with the blood that had pooled in his groin to coax his hands higher.

The contact of warm flesh on his rough fingers had them both gasping as he tunneled his hands under her shirt. He groaned into her mouth when he found her naked beneath it and skimmed his hands slowly up her ribs until the full weight of her breasts brushed the backs of his knuckles.

He felt her shiver when he grazed the tips of those glorious breasts with his thumbs, felt them peak and, grinding his hips hard against hers, thrust his tongue deeper into her mouth. She sighed into him, opening wider, inviting him deeper still, as he squeezed and caressed and wished to hell there wasn't a little girl about to come tripping down the stairs any minute and expect him to take her for a horseback ride.

"Peg...darlin'," he murmured on a frustrated groan and reluctantly broke the contact of their mouths. Breathing hard, he dragged his hands out from under her shirt and wrapped her tightly in his arms. Then it was his turn to shiver, to draw a shaky breath. "We...oh, man...we got a little carried away there, baby."

He felt the moment she came back to herself. Felt the stiffness of her shoulders, the awareness of what they'd just shared hit home.

He was smiling drowsily when she pulled away from him. Until he saw her face.

"Damn you," she whispered, barely able to get the words out. "Damn you for that."

He'd expected a little anger—at least a token

show—even though he knew that she'd enjoyed it as much as he had.

What he hadn't expected was shame. But that's what she felt, he realized grimly, as her eyes brimmed with tears and the flush desire had painted on her cheeks faded to a ghostly pale.

"Peg?" He touched a hand to her arm. "Hey. It was just a kiss, darlin'."

She jerked away.

"Whoa now, no need for that," he coaxed softly about the same time that he heard widget cowboy boots clumping down the stairs.

He backed a step away and Peg whirled away from him, pressed her hands to her cheeks. And all Cutter could do was stare and wonder about her reaction and why she looked so bruised.

"I'm ready," Shelby announced from the kitchen doorway. She was all decked out in a lavender hat, plaid shirt, blue jeans and, of course, her battered red boots. "Mom...how come you don't have your jeans on?" she asked, sounding put out. "Hurry up, silly."

"Let me...let me just put these dishes in the sink to soak," Peg said, her voice tight and a little shaky.

"I can do that," Cutter said, suddenly feeling like a heel when what he'd wanted to feel was a little more of Peg pressed against him.

"You go get changed," he added, not surprised when she shouldered around him at a fast walk then took the stairs at a trot.

"Come on, Shelby Lynn," she said over her shoulder. "Help me find my riding boots."

Cutter watched the little girl roll her eyes and shrug

her shoulders as if to say, ''Moms. They are so scatterbrained.'' Calling the dog, she trotted along after her mother.

And Cutter was left to smile after them, then frown at the red ribbon in his hand. He resisted the temptation to stuff it in his pocket and laid it on the counter instead. Then he cleared up the table, dumped the dishes in the sink and ran some water over them. Shoving his fingers in his hip pockets, he headed thoughtfully down to the barn to check out the tack situation.

He hadn't wanted to hurt Peg. He'd just wanted to kiss her. Just once for old times' sake. Just once to see if his memory had been bigger than the reality.

Now he knew. His memory didn't even begin to compare with the real live perfection of Peg Lathrop's mouth. Or her long, lithe body pressed against his like a firebrand. Or the softness of her breasts warm and heavy in his hands.

Well, so much for what he'd wanted, he decided, opening what he figured was the tack-room door. He'd go for a ride with them—because he'd promised the little girl that he would. Then he'd get out of Dodge. Now that he knew he'd hurt Peg six years ago, he didn't want to hurt her again. And if he stuck around much longer that's just what he'd do. He'd hurt her because now he knew something else. Something that he hadn't known before. He wanted more from Peg than a kiss—and then she'd want something more from him, too. Peg would want forever. She deserved it, too, but...damn...even if he wanted to, he'd figured out a long time ago that forever was something he just didn't have in him to give.

When Peg worked up the courage to leave the house, she spotted both her sorrel gelding, Henry, and Shelby's POA, Bea, saddled and bridled, their reins looped over a fence rail. Cutter was just leading Jackpot out of the barn.

She made herself breathe deep, tried to forget about what had happened in her kitchen. What she'd *let* happen.

Damn.

Damn. Damn. Damn.

She wasn't even sure how he'd managed it. One minute she'd been laying into him about something he'd said and then the next he'd had her backed up against the sink and was kissing her like there was no tomorrow.

And she'd kissed him back.

That was the worst part. She'd stood there, wanting him to leave her alone, and with one touch of his mouth to hers, she'd been just plain wanting. Wanting him. Naked. Inside her.

Even now, she went all wobbly and weak thinking about his mouth and his tongue. In her mouth. She hadn't even gotten past the shiver when she remembered the feel of his hands—in her hair, on her breasts. And his body pressed up against her. Hard, hot...and ready to take that kiss a whole lot further.

She blew out a breath, flexed her fingers. Shook it off. "That's what you get for living the life of a spinster," she muttered.

And that's what this was all about. This wasn't about Cutter. This was about her physical needs that she'd denied for, well, let's just say a very long time. Okay. Six years to be exact. She could have kicked herself right now for that oversight.

It wasn't that she hadn't had offers. Some of them had even included marriage. None of them had been right. Not for her. Not for Shelby.

"Like Cutter *is* right?" she sputtered under her breath as she neared the barn. No. Cutter was nothing but wrong. He was also too gorgeous for his own good—or obviously for hers.

Well, she was prepared for him now. No more surprises because this time she really did have his number. Alley cat. Love 'em and leave 'em. All she had to do was remember that and not get caught up in his slow, suggestive grins or his hot, hungry looks.

Fortunately he wasn't looking at her when she reached Henry and gathered the reins in her hands. He was very studiously helping Shelby get settled on Bea's back, checking her stirrup length, making sure she had a good handle on the reins.

Averting her gaze, she swung up into the saddle. Then she made a conscious effort not to dwell on the picture the two of them made—Shelby and Cutter—with their heads together, hers adoring, his amused.

"Ready?" he said, never once looking her way.

"It'd probably be best if you led Jackpot away from the barn a bit. If he blows, I'd just as soon he didn't take you through the barn door."

He glanced up then, looking a little encouraged, apparently thinking that she had his welfare in mind.

"I don't have the time or the money to handle a repair bill," she added to make sure she nipped that little notion in the bud.

He ducked his head, shook it, then gathered Jackpot's reins and led him out to the field behind the barn. She kept Shelby beside her and both of them a careful distance away while they waited until Cutter mounted. She really had no idea what the fiery little paint would pull.

Instead of swinging right into the saddle, Cutter took his time inspecting his tack, double-checking the bit, talking softly to the gelding who alternately laid back his ears and flicked them forward as if he were really interested in hearing what the cowboy had to say.

Oh, he was interested all right, Peg thought. Interested in finding the right moment to take a chomp out of Cutter. A part of her relished the possibility and yet her conscience got the best of her. "He's a biter. Watch your back."

Cutter looked up, surprised at her warning. A hopeful grin jacked up one side his mouth.

"Can't afford a vet bill, either," she said, clarifying that she was worried about what would happen to the horse if he bit into tainted meat.

Cutter just shook his head again, tugged down his hat and gathered the reins. He swung up and into the saddle so effortlessly that it took a moment for Peg to realize that Jackpot was still standing there as docile as a kitten. Only his laid-back ears gave away that he was not a happy horse.

"Stay back a bit," Cutter suggested. "Let the two

of us come to an understanding before you crowd him.''

That was just fine with Peg. And Shelby was enough of a cowgirl to understand the importance of following an order. Rascal ran in happy circles around Henry and Bea as they started off at a slow walk several yards behind Cutter and Jackpot.

"Told you he could ride him," Shelby said after they'd gone about a tenth of a mile.

Peg smiled for her little cowgirl, working hard to conceal an irritation that had no place in Shelby's world. "Yeah, punkin', you sure did."

"I like him. Do you think he likes me?" her daughter asked with such hope that Peg felt the bend, then the break of her heart. It also reminded her that keeping her cool wasn't really about her unwanted attraction to Cutter. It was about something much more important. It was about her little girl's heart.

"Sure he does, sweetie. What's not to like?" she added with a lightness she didn't feel and a weight in her chest that made it difficult to draw a deep breath.

Why wouldn't a daddy love his little girl?

She blinked back a sudden mist of tears. Tears of guilt. Of anger. What kind of justice made a mother withhold a father from his daughter to keep from hurting her and in the same breath wonder if her deception might be hurting her more.

Four

"**H**e doesn't much like the bit," Cutter said about Jackpot as the three of them, with Rascal scampering eagerly at their heels, headed toward the barn on their way back from their ride in the foothills.

"He responds much better to leg commands. And he respects authority. You keep that in mind, Peg, and you two will get along just fine."

Cutter glanced at Peg, who acknowledged his advice with a nod. He shook his head, tugged on his hat. They'd ridden the better part of two hours. Two pretty quiet hours—except for Shelby. Peg hadn't had much to say during the whole ride. Now little Shelby Lynn—she was another story altogether, Cutter thought with a grin. Her little-girl chatter and her insatiable curiosity about cowboys and rodeo had tickled the hell out of him.

They'd had a heated debate—one that he'd egged on just to get her going—over who was the best all-around cowboy of all time. She was determined it was Ty Murray. He was pretty much in agreement, but deliberately goaded her by declaring it was Joe Beaver.

"But he don't even ride wild horses," Shelby protested with an exaggerated roll of her eyes that relayed just how wrong she thought he was. "He ropes calves. Little bitty calves. Where's the danger in that is what I'd like to know."

He laughed and defended his position. "Takes a might lot of skill to rope and tie a calf."

She gave a derisive snort. "Yeah, right. Ty could rope a silly little calf if he wanted to. But I bet Joe couldn't ride a bronc—or a bull. You ever ride a bull, Cutter?"

"Do I look *that* stupid?" he asked her with an exaggerated show of horror.

"Well, when you picked Joe Beaver over Ty Murray, it kinda makes me wonder."

He chuckled. "The apple didn't fall too far from *your* tree," he said over Shelby's head to Peg, who seemed to turn a little pale before she found her voice.

"That's my girl." She managed a smile that Cutter noticed didn't hold much humor.

Well, he still didn't know what to make of things. He knew he'd really messed up coming on so hot and heavy in her kitchen earlier. But damn, just being around her seemed to leach the brains right out of his head and into that spot he'd been accused of thinking with far too often to make him proud.

Well, his brain was back in his head where it belonged now and it was telling him he needed to be moving on. Judging by the way Peg was acting, it couldn't be too soon to suit her.

"Whoa, now," he murmured to a suddenly skittish Jackpot when a stalk of bear grass tickled the paint's flank and had him crow-hopping into Shelby's POA. He jerked hard to the right, trying to pull Jackpot around and away from Bea, but the flighty gelding had decided he was good and spooked and wasn't about to be settled down.

Before it was over, Bea had bolted and was heading at a run for the barn. Shelby, he could see, was up to it. She was a natural in the saddle, had a good hold on her reins and her saddle horn as she yelled at Bea to, "Slow down, you goofy pony!"

Peg's gelding was levelheaded but a little fidgety, too, over all the activity. She had him well in hand as Jackpot danced on his back legs and struck out like a kindergartner scared silly in a Halloween haunted house.

Everything was fine. He was in control until Rascal, answering his natural herding instincts, decided he needed to help bring Jackpot to tow and dived in for a quick nip at his heels.

"Rascal, no!" Peg screamed—but too late.

The frenzied paint struck out with a powerful hind hoof, caught Rascal square in the ribs and sent him sailing.

"Damn," Cutter swore, and after several long minutes, finally got Jackpot settled down.

He bailed off and, leading a quivering and heaving

Jackpot, trotted to Rascal's side. Peg was on her knees in the grass beside him.

"Damn," he said again as he went down on one knee. "Where'd he get him?"

Peg looked up through tear-misted eyes. "In the chest. Oh, Cutter, he's barely breathing."

Cutter swiped a hand over his jaw. He glanced over his shoulder and saw that Shelby had seen what happened and was reining Bea back out toward them. He didn't want her to see this.

"Keep him down. Stay with him and try not to let him move," he ordered then he snagged Henry's reins from Peg and swung into her saddle. "I'll get the horses settled and come back for you in my pickup."

"Hurry." A tear tracked down her cheek.

"He'll be fine," he said and wished to hell he knew if he was telling it straight. "He'll be just fine."

Then he cued Henry into a jog and, leading Jackpot by the reins, headed off toward Shelby.

"Come on, Shelby," he said when he met her in the middle of the field. "Let's get these horses settled real quick and then we need to get Rascal to the vet."

"Is he dead?" she wailed, tears pouring down her face. "Did Jackpot kill him?"

"No, darlin'. He's not dead. But he's hurt real bad so we need to be brave and act fast now, are you hearing me?"

Shelby bit her lower lip and nodded as the tears kept flooding down—and Cutter's heart just flat out broke.

"There's my girl. Now you go turn Bea into the paddock and pull off her tack, okay? Then you make sure there's water in the tank while I turn out the other horses. Can you do that for me?''

She nodded and headed for the barn at a fast trot with him right on her heels.

Damn. He hated this. He hated the look on Peg's face. He hated the worry in little Shelby's blue eyes. He hated that that darn little dog may have nipped at his last set of heels.

But most of all, he hated that he was the best thing the two Lathrop girls had going for them at the moment. It didn't say too much about their luck—and less about his opinion of himself than he'd ever care to admit.

When Peg came out of the examining room, they were sitting side by side on the chairs in the veterinary clinic's waiting room. The man and the child. Father and daughter.

In the few moments before Cutter looked up and saw her, the picture the two of them made together burned into Peg's mind in a way that she knew would haunt her forever.

It was a picture she'd never confessed to anyone that she'd imagined before. Many times. In the dark of night. In bed alone. Or when Shelby had been a baby, cutting a tooth, running a temp on a cold, quiet, winter midnight and the rocking chair, a loving hand and her breast had been the only comfort Peg had to offer. In those times, when no one else knew, she would indulge in her fantasies, and wallow in regrets. She would picture them together, wonder at the fit.

She didn't have to wonder any longer. The man

she'd pictured had been younger, leaner, greener. The man who sat with her daughter was more now than he'd been back then. More than Peg had figured he'd ever become.

Cutter's dark head was bent over Shelby's, one big hand stroking her baby girl's downy soft blond hair. His other hand, gentle and scarred and strong, rested carefully and protectively on Shelby's small shoulders. The two of them were oblivious to her standing there watching them. Their blue eyes were locked, his compassionate and comforting, hers worshipful and trusting.

With her heart in her throat, Peg touched trembling fingers to her lips and tried to hold herself together by banding her other arm around her waist. Picturing them together on a long lonely night was one thing. Seeing them together was another. It made her question not only her decision, but also made her question her motives.

Oh, Shelby. What have I done?

"Hey," Cutter said softly when he looked up and saw her standing in the doorway. "How's it going back there?"

Peg forced a smile for Shelby. "Good. It's going good. He's going to be okay."

Shelby shot off the chair and ran to her mother. Peg scooped her up, hugged her hard against her.

"Can we take him home now?"

Peg pressed a kiss to the top of Shelby's head, smelled her sweet little-girl scent—and the faint scent of Cutter's aftershave that made her think of dry fall grass and leather. "Not just yet, cupcake. Rascal's got a couple of broken ribs so he's pretty sore. The doc wants to keep him overnight to make sure nothing else turns up.''

"He could get sicker?'' Shelby wailed.

"No. No, sweetie.'' She ran a comforting hand over her cheek. "That's why he's going to stay here tonight. To make sure that doesn't happen. We can pick him up tomorrow, okay?''

"Okay.'' Shelby's frown deepened. "Darn Jackpot. He was a bad horse.''

"Jackpot was just scared, Shell,'' Cutter said, and Peg watched him stand, unfolding in one smooth, graceful motion and walk over to them. "You ever get scared?''

Shelby was tired and still a little upset. Peg could tell that she was winding up to get just a little cranky. And why not? She'd had a bad scare.

"No,'' Shelby insisted anyway. "I don't get scared, do I, Mom?''

Before she could respond, Cutter did. "What about today? Were you scared when Rascal got hurt?''

Shelby buried her face in her mom's neck rather than admit that she'd been good and scared.

"Well, the way I figure it, you were and now you're mad at Jackpot. Just like Jackpot was scared and he got mad at Rascal for nipping at him. I'm sure Jackpot's sorry.''

While Shelby was thinking that over, Peg was wishing that *she* didn't have so much to think about. Like the fact that she felt grateful to Cutter for his gentle explanation. He'd been careful of Shelby's feelings, recognized that she was acting out her distress. He was a natural, she realized. A natural father.

She closed her eyes as guilt took a deeper gouge out of the hole it had been eating in her stomach ever since he'd shown up in Sundown.

"I don't suppose anyone's hungry but me." Cutter tilted a grin Shelby's way.

On cue, Peg's stomach growled. It had been a long time since breakfast. She hadn't even thought about it until now. She glanced at the wall clock. It was almost one o'clock.

Shelby was still feeling a little pouty. "Not hungry."

"Hmm." Cutter pinched his chin between his thumb and fingers. "And here I was all tuned up for a super-duper double Bozeman burger." He lifted a brow, angled Shelby, who was still hugging her mom, a pointed look.

"And French fries?" Shelby asked into Peg's shirt.

"And a chocolate malt, if you want one," Cutter added and Peg could feel her daughter's cheeks plump up into a grin.

"All right!" Shelby exclaimed, and suddenly having her fill of pouting squirmed out of Peg's arms and ran to Cutter.

He didn't even hesitate when Shelby lifted her arms. He just scooped her up, settled her on his hip and looked expectantly at Peg. "You coming, Mom?"

The fatigue that had set in over Rascal's ordeal regrouped into a panic so profound, it made her tremble. She did not want to do this. She did not want to see this. She did not want to watch her daughter with Cutter and know that she and she alone was responsible for them never being together until now. She did not want to sit beside him on the hour-long trip to Bozeman to get a super-duper double Bozeman burger, fries and a chocolate malt. And agonize over whether she should just tell him.

"Thanks, Cutter, but I...I don't think that's such a good idea."

"It's a *great* idea, Mom! It's been *forever* since we've gone to Bozeman," Shelby wheedled.

Her eyes were bright again. She'd already forgotten her fear for Rascal. And what Cutter was suggesting was a kind and caring way of keeping that fear at bay.

What could she do, what could she say but, "Okay. We go to Bozeman. Satisfied?"

"Yea!" Shelby cried and laughing, wrapped her little arms around Cutter's neck as if she'd been hugging him and loving him her entire life.

Peg looked at her hands, ignored her pounding heart and composed herself. "Well, let's get this show on the road then."

And then she followed them out the door, wishing with everything in her that she was as sure today as she'd been just yesterday of a decision she'd made long ago that had set the course of all their lives.

Cutter sat across from Peg and Shelby in the yellow plastic booth with the red tabletop and salt and pepper shakers shaped like fat little hamburgers and wondered what the hell he was doing with these two *women*.

Sure, one was about as big as a pint of ice cream, but she had a woman's way about her—at least she did with him. He'd never given much thought to kids before, yet little Shelby Lynn Lathrop had wrapped him around her little finger in about the same amount of time it took Joe Beaver to rope and tie a calf.

And then there was the other one.

The other one, looking good enough to eat and as tense as a bull rider's rope, was sitting across from him in the booth. She'd made a great show of working on her burger and fries and occasionally sipping from Shelby's malt, but the truth was she'd hardly eaten a thing.

Okay. So he'd surprised them when he'd stuck his neck out and invited them out for a burger. Hell, he'd surprised himself and was still wondering what on God's green earth had possessed him.

The same thing that had possessed him this morning when he'd headed for her place instead of out of town. Yeah, he'd made a mistake looking up Peg this morning, a bigger mistake kissing her. Then he'd compounded it by going on that ride. Things hadn't been beyond fixing, though, and he hadn't been beyond getting at that point, until Rascal had pulled his stunt. Well, what could he have done then? Just tip his hat, wish them luck with the dog and head on out? No. Wasn't his style.

Then at the vet's he'd gotten in deeper and deeper. That poor little girl. She'd been worried sick. Those big fat tears that had welled then spilled down her cheeks—man. It had just torn him up.

Of course he'd had to comfort her. And when all was well, he'd been so relieved he'd felt like celebrating. Besides, a man had to eat and he *had* been hungry. So had they. The invitation had just popped out. It had been worth it, too—just to see little Shelby perk back up and smile for him.

It was a killer smile. Melted his heart right down to a puddle of mush, that's for sure. Just like looking at her momma did other things to his body that didn't have a thing to do with his heart—at least he didn't think so.

Anyway, that's how he'd ended up still hanging around when he ought to be heading his truck down the highway. That reminded him. He'd seen a pay phone back by the men's room. He needed to cancel a hot date with a wild bronc. He blew out a breath, scratched his head and resettled his hat. He'd just as well have tossed *that* entry fee out a window.

"I gotta make a quick call, Peg, then we can go, okay?"

"Sure," she said.

"Then can we go to the movies, Cutter?" Big blue eyes looked into his with a plea that could have stripped the locks on Fort Knox.

"Shelby Lynn," Peg admonished. "Where are your manners? Cutter was nice enough to drive us here for a burger and now you're trying to take advantage of his kindness."

Cutter couldn't help it. He smiled into those baby blues. He knew he was being played for a sucker and somehow he didn't mind a bit. "You want to see a movie, sugar?"

"Oh, could we, Cutter? It's been *forever* since I got to see a movie."

Cutter sliced Peg a look. She just rolled her eyes and shook her head over her daughter's antics.

"Only if it's okay with your mom."

"As if I really had a say in this," Peg mumbled.

"Yea! We get to go to a movie. We get to go to a movie," Shelby singsonged, happily dipping a French fry into her glob of ketchup then stuffing it into her mouth.

It was dark by the time they turned down Peg's road because after the movie—some silly, sweet little animated adventure about dogs and cats and of all things, pigs—they'd *had* to go out for pizza. Because, well, it had been *forever* since Shelby Lynn had been to her favorite pizza place and because Cutter seemed to be a pushover for anything Shelby set her mind to convincing him that she needed.

Peg looked down on the child who had fallen asleep in her arms before they'd cleared the Bozeman city limits. Her daughter had the face of a baby cherub and the instincts of a grifter suckering in her prey. She smiled in the dark, adjusted Shelby's soft, warm weight and let out a contented sigh—then blinked and brought herself to attention when she realized what had happened.

She'd gotten comfortable. Comfortable with the idea of sitting in the cozy cab of Cutter's truck with Cutter behind the wheel, the radio playing softly, and their daughter asleep in her arms. And it scared her near to death.

She could not get comfortable with Cutter or with these fuzzy little notions about coming clean—just blurting out between a Garth Brooks and a Faith Hill song that Shelby was his child.

She could *not* get comfortable at the thought of the two of them walking into her little house and tucking Shelby into bed—then whispering their way down to her own bedroom and…and—

"—Peg?"

She jerked, blinked and realized that they were parked in her driveway. Cutter had cut the engine. He was staring at her, his eyes questioning across three feet of moonlight-dusted cab.

"I'm sorry," she whispered. "Did you say something?"

"Yeah," he said, looking puzzled. "I said sit tight. I'll come around and get her, carry her into the house for you, okay?"

"No. No," she said abruptly. "I can get her."

But he was already out of the truck. And then he was opening her door. And the next thing she knew, he was sliding his arm under Shelby's shoulders—which just happened to involve brushing against her breasts. And then his other arm was under Shelby's legs—which just happened to involve brushing against her thighs. And his face was just inches from hers in the summer night—which just happened to involve looking at him. At his brilliant blue eyes, his heartbreaker face, his lush, mobile mouth that wasn't smiling as he studied her with a dark, dangerous intensity that stole her breath.

She swallowed hard, worked even harder to keep a coherent thought as her blood took a notion to pound like thunder in her ears.

"I've got her," he said softly, never taking his gaze from hers, lingering with her daughter cradled in his arms and her body wedged beneath them.

So close. He was so close and he smelled so good and the night and the dome light were casting wonderful shadows across his jaw, defining and spotlighting the most intriguing little scar that hooked the left corner of his mouth that she'd never noticed before. Just like she'd never noticed that she could breathe with her heart jammed up in her throat the way it was.

"Peg? You okay?"

"What? Oh. Yeah. Yeah, I'm fine. Have you got her?"

"I've got her," he said, and lifted her baby girl into his arms.

For the longest time, all she could do was sit there. The heat of the July day had faded to a pleasant summer cool. Yet her palms were sweating as she watched Cutter's long, strong body, his effortless stride as he carried Shelby as if she were as fragile as glass, yet as if he'd carried her a hundred times, just like this.

And she didn't know what she was going to do.

He was almost to the porch steps when she realized that the one thing she couldn't do was sit there. She forced herself out of the truck, caught up with and passed him, then opened the front door so he could ease Shelby inside.

"Just put her on the sofa," she said when she'd flipped on the hall light.

"That's silly," he whispered over Shelby's head. "You'll just have to pick her up again and carry her up the stairs. Point me to her room and I'll put her to bed."

Okay. He was right. It made sense. And she could do this. "Top of the stairs. First door on the left."

He headed up the stairs and she stood at the bottom looking up. At a father carrying his daughter to bed.

She couldn't go up there—and she couldn't not go up there.

Cutter had already laid the rag doll that Shelby had turned into in the middle of her little bed by the time she'd trailed them up the stairs. Peg moved around him and tugged off Shelby's boots and socks. Then she carefully stripped down her jeans and peeled off her shirt until she was lying in her little T-shirt and panties dotted with pink flowers.

"She's good for the night," she whispered. She covered her with a sheet then brushed the hair back from her face and pressed a kiss to her brow. "G'night, darling girl," she murmured and trailed the back of her hand across Shelby's cheek.

Then she straightened and backed right into the hard, strong body that stood in silence behind her.

She froze. So did he as his big hands wrapped around her upper arms to steady her. She could feel his solid heat a faint heartbeat away from her back, the soft warmth of his breath feathering at her nape.

And just when her heart told her that he was going to turn her in his arms and take—not ask for—another kiss, he squeezed gently and let his hands drop away.

"She's a sound sleeper, huh?" he said in a hushed voice.

Peg closed her eyes, gathered her wits. "Yeah. She could sleep through a buffalo stampede."

An eternity passed as they stood there in the dark with their heartbeats and their shallow breaths and a soft spill of light shining into the room from the hallway.

"You're a good momma, Peg."

She hugged herself, braced. *Don't ask me. Don't, don't, don't. Please don't ask me.*

The night grew so heavy and so full of the possibility that she actually jumped when he drew a deep breath and touched his hand to her arm.

"I've got to go, okay?"

"Yeah," she said quickly and wondered at the feeling of loss when moments ago she'd thought the only good thing that could happen was that he leave. "Yeah. It's okay."

On stiff legs, she turned and walked out of the room, down the stairs and out onto the porch. She had to get some fresh air. The house suddenly felt stifling and closed in and the air so thick she was drowning in the suffocating, heavy weight of it.

She heard the screen door creak open and shut as Cutter joined her there where she stood with her back to the house and her arms wrapped tightly around her middle. If he touched her, she was lost. If he kissed her, she was gone.

"Peg—"

"—You'd better go."

A long silence passed. She could feel him watching her, sense him studying her.

"Are you afraid of me, Peg?" he asked in a voice that said he hoped not, he really, really hoped not.

It was his honest entreaty that prompted hers. "It's…it's just not a good idea for us…for us to be here. Like this."

Another silence, thick with questions, heavy with the only obvious conclusion. "Because of what it might lead to?"

"Yeah," she admitted quietly. "Because of what it might lead to." She looked over her shoulder at him. "Does it make you happy to know that?"

She hadn't meant to bite the last part out. But she'd never meant to admit her attraction, either, so she figured she was entitled to a little bite.

"It might," he said softly, "if it didn't seem to make you so sad."

She couldn't respond to that. Not without giving more of herself away. She already felt as if she'd stripped to the skin. So she said nothing. Tried to feel nothing.

"Well," he said, sounding sorry and resigned but determined to do as she asked. "Tell Shelby goodbye for me, will you? Tell her—tell her that I think she's quite the little cowgirl."

She nodded into her chest. The apple hadn't fallen too far from the tree, he'd said. What would you do, Cutter, if you knew? If you really knew?

She couldn't look at him. "Sure. I'll tell her. Goodbye, Cutter."

"Yeah," he said and she could feel his thoughtful gaze. "I guess it is."

After a long moment, his booted foot hit the second step. He stopped, drew a deep breath. "Look—it's been good seeing you," he finally said, his voice sounding rusty, as if he was having trouble getting those particular words out—as if there were other words he wanted to say but those were the ones that had come out anyway.

"You, too." She cut him a quick glance, then looked back at the night. At the truck that would be pulling out soon and never return to Sundown again. "Um—thanks for what you did today." She owed him this. "It...it was a nice thing to do for...for Shelby's sake."

He didn't say anything for the longest moment— so long that she couldn't stand it. She looked up at him, at those blue eyes that he'd given to her daughter.

"And what about her momma? Was it a nice thing I did for her, too?"

His eyes were searching. For forgiveness? For encouragement? For what, she didn't know. But it seemed important to him that she wasn't angry with him anymore. And suddenly, it seemed important to her that she wasn't angry anymore, either.

"Yes," she said and found that it wasn't so hard to smile. "It was a nice thing you did for me, too. I appreciated it. All of it."

All of it. Including the kiss. And right or wrong,

foolish or wise, she wanted him to kiss her again. That's why he had to leave. Before he kissed her again because if he kissed her again, she wouldn't want to let him go.

Yet as they stood there, with a soft wind blowing, a night owl calling, and a dusty miller flitting around the porch light, she was sure that he was going to. His gaze sought hers, searched. His hand reached out, touched her cheek, then slowly dropped away. With a long, lingering look, he turned and ambled in his loose-hipped cowboy walk, down the rest of the steps.

"You take care now, you hear?" he said over his shoulder.

She walked to the edge of the porch, hugged a post against her cheek where his hand had been. "I hear, Cutter. I hear."

Then she watched him climb into his truck and drive away.

Five

Cutter thought about driving all night long. Just stopping at the hotel, grabbing his gear and heading out under the big Montana sky. He was in a mood for driving. And Lord knew, he was good at leaving. But he went back to his hotel room, flopped down on the bed instead and folded his arms behind his head.

And he thought about Peg. About how he'd finally gotten the smile he'd been looking for. About how her generous heart had finally forgiven him for sins he should have known he'd committed but had only owned up to today.

He thought about that sweet little blue-eyed girl who didn't have a daddy. And then he made himself think about something else because he did not want to let his thoughts lead him down that road.

That led him right back to pretty Peg again. Soft

mouth. Soft breasts. It had been a long time but he still remembered the taste of her in his mouth. Velvet and silk. Roses and cream. He still remembered the way it felt to be inside her. Tight and pulsing, slick satin heat.

Yeah. He'd gone out there this morning hoping he'd get a little taste of Peg again. And he'd found out that she was a momma.

It had changed things. Kids always changed things. For one thing, it had made her an adult. A kid required that of a person. Made them grow up. Made them give up on their own dreams to cater to things like food and shelter. Money to pay bills.

That's why he'd always avoided any serious relationships. Serious led to responsibility. He wasn't ready for responsibility. He wasn't ready to grow up. Which meant he wasn't ready for Peg. Probably never would be. Hell, he was his old man's son, after all. Wayne Reno hadn't been able to stick around, had he? Cutter couldn't even remember the last time he'd seen him. He'd blow in, blow out, and leave his momma crying.

He rolled to his side, punched the pillow and tucked it under his bent arm. Cutter hated his old man. He hated him because of what he'd done to his mom—and what he'd done to him.

Mostly what he'd done had been to not be there. But when he was, it was even worse. He remembered one time in particular. He'd been six. His dad must have shown up in the middle of the night because he'd just been there that morning when Cutter had gotten up. His momma had had to work so Cutter had stayed with his dad—hoping, as only a child could hope—that there was some love lying behind those eyes that stared at him like he was an ant who'd invaded his private picnic.

"Come on, boy. Let's go git us somethin' to wet our whistle."

Hope. It had grown and swelled. His dad wanted to take him somewhere. Maybe if he was real good, real quiet, he'd see that he was a good boy. He'd want to stay this time.

"Cute kid," the lady behind the bar with the bright red lips and baggy eyes had said.

"That one there?" his dad had glanced over his shoulder at him then laughed into his beer. "Hell, that one there was just an accident—and now him and his momma are like a ball and chain round my lily-white neck, know what I mean?"

Cutter hadn't known what he'd meant, not then. He'd known that he hadn't felt happy anymore and the next day, his dad was gone again. A few years later, he'd finally figured out exactly what good old *Dad* had meant. Just like he'd had a better understanding of why his mom had cried at night.

He sat up abruptly. He hadn't been down that lost highway in a long time. He didn't much like going there now. He checked the clock, dragged a hand through his hair and bolted off the bed. Then he packed his things, checked out and was on the road within fifteen minutes.

And then he just drove. With the windows down and the radio up, he drove and he didn't look back. Not to his childhood. Not to Sundown. Not to pretty

Peggy Lathrop with the beautiful breasts and the strong, giving heart.

Not to the little blue-eyed cowgirl who hadn't had a daddy in *forever*.

"You miss her, don't you?"

Peg shoved her fork around on her plate and looked across the table into the sparkling violet eyes of Ellie Savage. "Yeah. I miss her, but Mom called last night so I got to talk to her."

"And?" Ellie prompted just as someone punched a quarter in the jukebox and an old Brooks and Dunn tune blared out, loud and bouncy.

"And she's having a blast. They went to the zoo yesterday. Sea World tomorrow and Sunday, it's the ocean."

Peg leaned back, looked around. The dinner crowd at the Dusk to Dawn—Sundown's one and only restaurant, bar and youth center all rolled into one—was thinning out. The party people were starting to filter in to belly up to the bar, tip back a few longnecks and wait for the band to start playing.

Ellie waved to John Tyler, one of the local boys, when he walked in the door. John came grinning over to the table to talk with the three of them. Peg smiled, listened with half an ear, and tried not to miss Shelby.

She'd debated about letting Shelby go with her folks for their annual two-week summer trip to visit Jack's brother's family in San Diego. Shelby was only five, after all. But her mom and Jack wanted to take her so badly and Shelby hadn't been to a zoo in *forever*. It was already the end of July and in a little more than three weeks, her baby girl would be starting kindergarten. So, she'd relented. And now she was lonely.

That's why she'd agreed to meet Lee and Ellie here at the Dusk to Dawn for dinner. Shelby had only been gone four days and her little house seemed as empty as a tomb.

"How are you doing with Jackpot?" Lee asked when John moved on over to the bar where a couple of his buddies had lured him over with the promise of buying him a beer.

She didn't look at Jackpot these days without seeing Cutter astride him.

"Fine, actually," she said, quickly drawing herself away from that picture and flashing Lee a smile. "He's really a great horse. It was like you said, he just needed some attention."

She'd been giving him plenty of it, too. With Shelby gone, she'd been spending her evenings in the barn or riding. And Jackpot really was coming along.

Feeling restless, she glanced around the large, open room with its scuffed wood floor, worn-out booths and brass-and-oak bar that looked like it came straight out of an Old West saloon. Then she watched distractedly as the band started setting up in the corner near the dance floor. When her attention returned to the table, Lee and Ellie were grinning at each other and Ellie's hand had disappeared beneath the table.

"You two need to get a room?" Peg teased.

They were little more than newlyweds. The special thing about their relationship was that the two of them had found each other. Lee had come home to Sundown a year ago to take care of Ellie and they'd ended up falling in love.

"We have a secret," Ellie whispered with a pretty blush.

Peg cocked her head. "So...tell."

"We're going to try to have a baby."

Peg looked from Ellie, who was radiant, to Lee, who looked a little green around the gills. She understood why. He was worried. Ellie, for all her exuberance and optimism, was taking a risk trying to get pregnant. While Ellie was one of the most well-adjusted people she knew, Ellie was also epileptic. Peg couldn't begin to comprehend the physical and emotional pain Ellie had endured coming to terms with and living with her condition.

But she did know one thing. Lee Savage was the best thing that had ever happened to her—just like Ellie was the best thing that had happened to him.

"So," Peg said, a little worried for Ellie herself, but determined not to burst her bubble, "trying's half the fun, huh?"

Lee snorted.

Ellie laughed. "I'll say."

They all laughed then and Peg could have cried for the look of love in Lee's eyes when his gaze locked on Ellie's across the table.

"It'll be all right," Ellie whispered.

Lee nodded. Closed his eyes. "It'll be fine," he said at last. "Doc says it will be fine, so it will be."

"Well," Peg said, her eyes twinkling, "guess that means you won't be staying for the dance."

And they didn't. They left shortly after and Peg,

thrilled for her friend's happiness but feeling even more lonely because of it, was left to debate what she was going to do with the rest of her night. She'd just decided she might as well go home when Krystal and Sam walked in.

"Well, lookie, lookie here. Peg, darlin', you out kickin' up your heels tonight?" This from Sam, a big bear of a man who loved his wife, his son and the opportunity to tease, in equal measure.

"Look at her, Krystal," he said tugging on his tan Stetson then making a twirling motion with his finger encouraging Peg to show him all the angles. "She's just as pretty as a picture. Didn't know you owned a dress, Peg. Looks real nice on you, too."

Krystal gave her husband a little shove. "Stow it, you big goon. You've seen Peg in a dress lots of times. At church," she added when he made a big show of crinkling his brows and scratching his head.

"Krystal, sweetheart, a church dress and *that* dress shouldn't even be mentioned in the same sentence. Hot, Peggy. Real hot," he added with a brotherly wink and ambled over to the bar.

Peg rolled her eyes and Krystal grinned. "He's right, you know. You do look pretty hot. Special occasion?"

"Yeah. My good jeans were dirty."

She was starting to feel self-conscious. It was just a dress. Just a pale yellow, gauzy little sundress. She'd fallen in love with it when she'd taken Shelby to the dentist in Bozeman last week. It was short and sassy and buttoned up the front of a bodice that nipped in at her waist and if she tugged just right, didn't show too much cleavage. Or maybe it did, judging from Sam's reaction.

"Is it too much, do you think?"

"Oh, honey," Krystal said with a laugh. "If I had the goods you've got, I'd show off the package, too."

"It's too much," Peg said and started for the door.

Laughing, Krystal grabbed her arm. "Oh, no, you don't. You aren't going anywhere. Now we got us a sitter for the night and Shelby's in California so you and me and Sam are gonna cut loose a little. I know I'm due. So are you.

"Margarita, Danny," she told the bartender as she dragged Peg along with her to the bar. "Two of them. Soon. You're looking at two women who've got some powerful thirsts."

"And a yen to get rowdy?" Sam asked hopefully as he tucked Krystal under one arm and Peg under the other.

His grin was infectious. So was Krystal's mood.

"Why not," Peg decided, feeling a little reckless. She couldn't remember the last time she'd let her hair down, acted anything but the part she'd been cast in as the responsible parent. Yes, it was a part she loved. But every once in a while…every once in a while, she just wanted to have fun. Looked like tonight she was going to get her chance.

She was hot. Her back was damp with perspiration, her hair clung to her temples. She'd danced almost every dance and she was breathless with laughter. The music was country and lively. The crowd was happy and loud. And thanks to the pitcher of margaritas Sam

had bought for her and Krystal, little John Tyler
didn't look nearly as young as he had an hour ago.
She was also starting to remember why she chose not
to be much more than a social drinker. The tequila
had gone straight to her head.

"How old did you say you were?" she asked with
a careful frown as John held her close and the band
slowed things down with a ballad.

She felt his smile against her hair where he'd
pressed his cheek. "Old enough for what you've got
in mind."

She pulled back, grinned. "It's the dress, right?"

"Oh, yeah," he said, grinning back, "the dress definitely did its part, but it's what's *in* the dress that's
got me goin'."

It was fun. The flirting, the dancing, even forgetting
that she was a mom for a little while and letting herself experience the attraction of a handsome man.

John Tyler was definitely that. He was also what
they called jailbait. He couldn't be more than twenty.
And even though he was pretty and even though she'd
had just enough to drink that she was of a mind to
end the long dry spell that had had her acting the fool
over Cutter Reno three weeks ago, it wasn't going to
end with John Tyler. It wasn't going to end with any
of the other cowboys who had offered up a dance—
or anything else she might have a need for tonight—
either.

Because they weren't right. And, as hard as she'd
worked trying to convince herself that she could do
it, because Peg wasn't cut from the cloth that thought
sex without love was better than nothing at all.

She'd traded her sexuality for motherhood six years ago. And that was fine. Well, it had *been* fine until Cutter had shown up again. It was his fault she was even thinking along those lines. Even knowing that taking up with him would have come to no good, she'd finally admitted to herself that she'd still wanted that cowboy. She'd been all itchy and achy ever since—and angry with herself for having such a loose hold on her hormones. And for letting herself feel a little lonely.

"Why don't you have a girlfriend, John?" she asked, looping her arms around his shoulders, accepting that she had to be content to simply be held for a little while by a warm, hard body and smiled at by a beautiful, interested face. In public. On a dance floor. With all of her clothes on.

"Because I've been waiting for you to notice me."

"Stop it. Truth, now. Why don't you have someone special?"

He shrugged, all cover-boy looks and cowboy charm. "I'm too young and ornery, I guess. I've got to finish school. Get settled somewhere."

"Somewhere that's not Sundown?"

Again, he shrugged. "Who knows. Maybe. In the meantime, what about you? Why don't you have a special guy in your life? And don't say it's because nobody's offered. You've got every single man within shouting distance dropping their jaws just thinking about you."

A loud crash sounded from the corner as a table toppled.

John never missed a beat. "There, see. Another jaw just hit the floor."

She laughed. "You're good for me."

The hand that was warm and strong at her waist squeezed then caressed. "I could be even better."

Oh, he was sweet. And oh, he was tempting—and she could see in his eyes that he was more than teasing. He was tempted, too.

"In another life, handsome," she said wistfully and since she figured she was only so strong she decided it was time to go home. Alone. She hugged him hard then kissed him softly on the cheek. "Thanks."

"For?" He held her hand as she made to pull away.

"For making me remember what it feels like to be a woman. Don't," she added on a laugh when his expression told her he could build on that feeling if she'd just agree to go somewhere dark and alone with him. "Don't even think it."

Then she turned to walk away—and ran right into the solid wall of Cutter Reno's chest.

Cutter had been watching Peg and the cowboy from just inside the door. Watching and scowling and feeling a heat that had less to do with the July night and the crush of partying bodies than it did with seeing that fancy-faced young stud putting the moves on Peg.

"Cutter," she finally said, clearly stunned to see him.

"That would be me."

She looked flustered. And flushed. And like she ought to be lying rumpled in the middle of a bed being made love to—by him—instead of standing in the middle of a room crowded with people.

Her eyes were a melting chocolate-brown. Her skin—and there was a whole hell of a lot of it showing above and below that sexy little excuse of a dress—was just as he remembered. A sweet, honeyed tan, misted with a dewy dampness that had his pulse leaping and his blood pooling to a part of his body that was very happy to see her.

"What...what are you doing here?" she finally asked, raising a hand to her throat where he could see her own pulse fluttering.

He ignored her question, asked one of his own. "Did I interrupt something?" He shot a glare toward the cowboy who had ambled back over to the bar, leaned against it and made a point of keeping an eye on Peg.

She blinked, glanced toward the bar, then back at him with an indignant, "What?"

"The kid? Did I interrupt something between you and junior?"

Oh, boy. He heard the edge of jealousy in his voice, felt the irritation prickle at the back of his neck in a spot right beneath his shirt collar—then he flushed red as a damn rose when she figured it out and laughed at him.

"Wait a minute. In the first place, you didn't tell me what you're doing here." She attempted to tick off her point but missed when she went to slap her index fingers together. "In the second place, what do you care?" She tried again for a check-off gesture.

Missed again. Undaunted, she gave it one more try. "And in the first place—"

"—Whoa now, darlin'. We've already been there," he interrupted with a laugh when it dawned on him that little Peg may have been partying very hardy before he'd wandered into the Dusk to Dawn looking for a beer and the guts to drive on out to her place to see her.

"That may be, but I still don't know what you're doing here."

He squinted down at her, not sure that he knew himself, and decided to play it light and breezy. "Peggy. Darlin'. How much have you had to drink?"

She sniffed and crossed her arms belligerently under her breasts. He damn near fell to his knees when that lush, soft flesh all but spilled out over the top of her dress.

"In the first place—"

His laughter cut her off.

"Okay, okay. So, maybe I've had one too many margaritas," she admitted with a little shrug that drew his undivided attention to the yellow cotton strap that slipped slowly off her left shoulder. "You might even go so far as to say I'm teetering just a little bit toward tipsy."

"Well, now," he drawled and digging deep for casual reached out and tugged her errant strap back into place. "Normally I like that in a woman."

"Well, now," she drawled right back, seemingly unmoved when his fingers lingered on her slender shoulder when it was all he could do to drop his hand

and not haul her flush against him. "I'll just bet you do."

She tried for a scowl but ended up answering his smile. Finally. Then just as fast, she looked away, her hand a little unsteady as she touched it to her hair, telling him that maybe she was a little rattled, too.

"I think maybe I need some air."

So did he. Between the smoke and the noise and her almost dress, he couldn't draw a breath that didn't feel like it was choking him.

Without a word, he took her by the arm and headed for the door. The muffled sound of a classic ballad floated over the heavy boom of the bass and the rumble of good-time laughter and followed them outside. He led her around the building toward the parking lot.

Their silent walk through the parked cars and pickups gave him the opportunity to think about her questions. Tipsy or not, she'd asked some damn good ones. The same ones he was asking himself. Why *was* he here? Why *did* he care? Since he didn't have any good answers, he asked one of his own.

"How's Rascal?"

"He's doing fine." She shot him a considering look that told him the fresh air was doing its job and clearing her head. "And you had a lot of nerve— paying my vet bill before you left town."

Technically he hadn't paid it before he'd left. He'd called the vet from Butte the next day then sent a check. "Yeah, a man could get hard time for pulling a stunt like that."

She stopped, faced him in the dimly lit lot. The summer breeze tugged at her hair. A silken strand caught at the corner of her mouth. "You didn't have to do that," she said softly.

"You could just say thanks." Unable to resist, he hooked a finger on the errant strand. He tugged it away from her face and tucked it behind her ear, his hand lingering longer than it should have before he let it drop away.

He'd felt her shiver, saw her throat work as she swallowed. "I...I could pay you back, too."

"No. You couldn't. Rascal wouldn't have gotten hurt if I hadn't stuck around."

"Oh, Cutter, it wasn't your fau—"

"—Just say thank you, Peg."

She angled her head, accepted that he wasn't budging and finally gave in. "Thank you, Peg."

He tipped back his head, smiled at the blanket of stars and her smart mouth. "Nice night."

"Hmm." She stopped by her old truck. Leaning back against it, her shoulder blades resting on the fender, she watched the sky with him. "Lover's moon."

He'd heard loud silences before. Those moments before the gate flew open and a bronc busted out into the arena, all lightning and strength and outrage. Those moments when a cowboy was down and the crowd sat hushed, waiting for movement, for a sign that everything was going to be okay. Those moments when a man knew that a woman understood what was on his mind.

Lover's moon. They'd made love beneath a moon like this. Hot love. Young love. Wild love.

He met her eyes, saw her searching, seeking, swallowing back a memory and a need he suspected was as strong as his own.

"How's Shelby?" he asked hoarsely.

"Fine." She looked quickly away. "She...she's fine."

He moved a step closer. Close enough to see the pulse skitter just beneath the dew-damp skin at her throat. Close enough to see a tiny, sexy smudge of mascara just below her left eye. Close enough to feel the warmth of her breath feather against his jaw. "Where's Shelby?"

She closed her eyes, was quiet a very long time before looking up and staring at a spot somewhere beyond his shoulder. "In California. With her grandparents."

He studied her face, saw what he'd dreaded, what he'd wanted, what he'd been craving since he'd left her a little over three weeks ago. He didn't know why he hadn't been able to get her out of his head. Was sure that coming back here was a mistake.

She didn't look like a mistake, though. She looked like every man's dream. She looked like a woman he wanted. And as he moved in closer, planted his palms on the fender at either side of her shoulders and caged her in, she looked like a woman who wanted a man.

"You know—I've missed two opportunities to dance with you." He leaned closer, whispered against her temple as he lowered his head. "Once on the Fourth and once...just now...inside. Will you dance with me, Peg?"

Music from the bar filtered softly outside and into the night. A steamy love song, a deep, driving beat.

He wasn't asking her to dance. They both knew what he was asking. And they both knew what other opportunities he'd missed. He could have stayed six years ago. A lot lately, he'd been wondering if maybe he should have. Her next words straightened him out on that notion.

"You shouldn't have come back, Cutter." Her voice was very soft and not at all sure but the moment she said it, he knew she was right. He shouldn't have come back. He'd known it when he'd lain awake every night since they last parted and ached for her. He'd known it when he'd climbed in his truck and headed down the highway to Sundown.

He'd known it and yet, here he was. And now that he was here, he wasn't going anywhere. Not unless she told him to leave. Not now that they were together, beneath the stars of this hot summer night where a distance of six years had shrunken to the few inches of moonlight standing between them.

There was still more she wanted to say. He could see it in so many telling little ways—the pulse that now fluttered like frightened butterfly wings at her throat, the unsteady rise and fall of her breasts, the pretty brown eyes that had grown shiny and a little wild.

"I told myself to stay away," he confessed, watching her eyes as he lowered his head to whisper against her mouth. "I told myself a hundred times that it was a bad idea to come back."

"Very…very bad," she agreed on a hushed murmur as her head fell back and she let his mouth wander.

Summer heat. Woman heat. He felt surrounded by it. Consumed with it. And the wanting to make love to her escalated to need.

"Be bad with me, Peg." The words whispered out on a low growl as he dragged his open mouth along her jaw then bent to that silky spot at the curve of her throat and slid his tongue over her wildly racing pulse. Her skin tasted of salt and seduction and sex. His mind reeled with a hundred ways he wanted to take her.

"Please." He nuzzled a path down her throat, wedged a knee between her thighs, felt her breath catch and her body quiver. An arrow of raw, sexual heat burned a path to his belly. "Be very bad with me."

Six

She wanted to. Oh, she wanted to, Peg admitted as Cutter's big, warm hands spanned her waist and drew her against his hips so she could feel how very, very bad he wanted to be.

And it shocked and excited and embarrassed her to realize that she might have crossed the line from wanting to wanton right then—right there in the Dusk to Dawn parking lot—if the sound of footsteps crunching over gravel and Krystal's concerned, "Peg? You out here, honey?" hadn't brought her to her senses.

She pushed Cutter away, drew a steadying breath.

"Over here, Krystal." She heard the huskiness in her voice, felt Cutter's gaze, dark and hot on her face.

Her heart was still racing when Krystal rounded Peg's truck. She stopped short when she saw Cutter—

looked from him to Peg then back to Cutter again. There was little doubt that she'd figured out exactly what they'd been doing—or about to do.

"Thought that was you I saw walk into the bar," Krystal said, watching Cutter thoughtfully.

"How's it going, Krystal?" Cutter leaned a shoulder against the fender and tucked his hands in his back pockets.

"It's goin' just fine. You?"

One corner of his mouth lifted in a tight smile—more grimace than grin. "Never better."

Again, she glanced from Peg to Cutter then demonstrated why she'd never been known for her subtly. "So, what brings you back to Sundown?"

Cutter locked his gaze on Peg's. It was so hot she felt the sizzle sear her cheeks. "Just a little unfinished business."

Krystal gave Cutter another hard stare and switched her attention to Peg. "You okay?" She looked as if she was trying to decide if this was a good thing or a bad thing, finding the two of them together.

Peg smiled uneasily. "I just needed some air. And now I think I'm going to call it a night. It's...it's getting a little late for me."

Krystal narrowed her eyes. "Can you drive okay?"

"I'm fine," Peg insisted. At least she thought she was. That kiss had been one sobering experience. One sobering, sensual, scary experience.

"I'll make sure she gets home all right," Cutter said, enough challenge in his voice to let Krystal know he didn't appreciate or need her interference.

Krystal stood there, clearly debating whether or not

she should do just that. "It's all right. Really," Peg added and shot Krystal a reassuring smile.

"We'll get your truck home, Peg—but you call me tomorrow, okay?" Krystal said after a long moment.

"Sure."

"You see to it," she heard Krystal say in a hushed voice, "that nothing bad happens to her."

Cutter acknowledged the warning with a nod. "Tell Sam I'll drop by to see him before I leave town again."

"You do that," Krystal said. She was still standing in the middle of the lot when Cutter walked Peg to his truck.

Peg's hands were shaking as she clamped them together in her lap. Her head was clear. She was sober now. Stone-cold sober—had been ever since Cutter had backed her up against her truck and kissed her like he wanted to eat her up in big, gulping bites.

She shivered and flushed hot and cold all at the same time as she glanced at him beside her in his truck's dark interior.

The reality of what was about to happen crept into the night by slow degrees. Did she really know what she was doing bringing this alley cat home with her? Krystal had made it clear that she wondered the same thing. Peg found it interesting that for all of Krystal's attempts to convince her that she should give Cutter another chance, tonight she seemed to have finally understood what Peg had known all along. Cutter didn't play for keeps. Cutter played for the sake of playing. Not out of meanness. He just liked to play.

Which was why she was still puzzled over why he'd come back to play with her.

Sundown was definitely off his regular flight path. She didn't doubt for a minute that he could have found any number of willing and eager partners without altering his course. So, no, she had no idea what had prompted him to come back. Was still trying to recover from the shock of it. And with the fact that she was letting him drive her home.

Her heartbeat quickened as he turned into her driveway. Because she was lonely, that's why, she admitted pragmatically. And because Shelby's absence had driven home a very salient point. She had no life other than the life she lived for her daughter. She'd made that life be enough. She was content for it to be enough. Most of the time. But for one night of that life, she wanted to live it for herself.

Did it make her selfish? Maybe. Did it make her irresponsible? Probably. She couldn't help but think that it also made her human. With human wants and human needs and for one night—*one night*—she was willing to forgive herself for taking what she wanted and damn the consequences.

She would have this night with Cutter Reno. She was entitled. And she was due. She'd use him just the way he intended to use her. For pleasure. For comfort. And, she admitted reluctantly, she'd use him to alleviate a stark, aching loneliness that had crept up on her tonight like a thief and stolen her ability to defend herself against it.

He pulled to a stop in front of her house, killed his lights and climbed out of the cab. Lowering her head to the back of the passenger seat, she closed her eyes and told herself it didn't hurt to know that when he'd gotten what he wanted, he'd be gone.

She would not fall in love with him all over again. Knowing he'd leave. Knowing this time that what had once felt like a promise of forever, was just another love-the-one-you're-with episode in his life.

Yes, he would leave her. But she'd survived the last time and she would survive again. And maybe, just maybe, in the morning, she'd have him out of her system—along with one more reason to confirm that she'd done the right thing by not telling him about Shelby.

Refusing to give in to the guilt or the uncertainty, she lifted her head, turned to see his blue eyes, serious and searching, gaze at her through the open truck window. He was so beautiful. So darkly handsome, so ruggedly male. She wanted to feel his strength over her, pumping into her. She wanted to feel his hands and mouth—everywhere.

This time, she was going to take as much from Cutter Reno as he was going to take from her. This time, her heart wouldn't be on the line because this time, she saw through the tender lies in his eyes that said he loved her.

And this time would have to be enough.

She told herself that the tightening she felt in her chest wasn't heartache. It was anticipation. Excitement. She was entitled. She was entitled to feel like a woman again. And she was woman enough to handle the goodbye.

When he opened her door for her, she drew a deep breath, took his hand and climbed out of the truck.

After bending down to give Rascal the hello pat he begged for and making sure he really was okay, Cutter followed Peg in silence as she walked ahead of him toward her little house.

See to it that nothing bad happens to her. Krystal's words played over and over in his head. Translation: Don't hurt her.

He didn't want to hurt anyone. He especially didn't want to hurt Peg but the closer he got to her door, the deeper it settled that that's exactly what he'd do if he spent the night.

He wished to hell that he didn't have such a big, bad need for her. He wished the gentle sway of her hips as she walked ahead of him didn't undercut his conscience and make him want her more. He wished that any number of women who were both willing and wise to his ways would have been enough to take his mind off this one woman.

Yeah, and he could wish in one hand and spit in the other and the result would be the same. He wanted her. And damn his selfish hide, there wasn't anything he could do to convince himself he wasn't going to have her. Unless she said no.

When she opened the screen door, he reached around her, flattened a palm against the frame above her head and pushed it shut. She turned slowly, leaned back against the door and met his eyes in the moon-drenched night.

He touched a finger to her cheek and searched her

face, her beautiful, wholesome face that he wanted to watch when he made her climax. "You can still say no."

She turned her face to the side. "Is that what you want me to say?"

He drew in a deep breath, then let it out. "Not in a million years."

"Then come inside."

She turned back toward the door. His hand on her arm stopped her.

"Why are you letting this happen?"

A flicker of uncertainty flashed in her eyes and then was gone. "Why are you asking so many questions? Why aren't you kissing me?"

"Because I want you to want this as much as I do." He counted heartbeats and waited for her reply. "Do you want me, Peg?"

She wet her lips with her tongue and nodded.

A fierce clutch of possession curled in his gut. "Say it. Say you want me."

Her eyes were dark. Her breasts rose and fell gently with each tremulous breath she drew. "I want you, Cutter. I've always wanted you."

He didn't need another invitation—he'd been waiting for this one for what seemed like his entire life. To hell with his conscience. It had never stood a chance anyway.

He pressed her into the screen door with his body, covered her mouth with his and took the kiss he'd been craving with a hard, hot assault of open mouth and seeking tongue. She was liquid and lush against him, the soft cushion of her breasts pressing into his chest and driving his hips into action.

She sucked in a sharp breath when he reached between them, his fingers quick and sure as he opened the top button on her dress.

"This dress…has been…driving me…crazy," he growled between hungry kisses and undid another button, shuddering when the soft warmth of her breasts brushed against the back of his knuckles.

"It's…new," she managed to say, sounding breathless and bothered then bent her knee and pressed against his other hand as he worked it beneath her skirt to caress her bare thigh.

"This dress…ought to be…outlawed," he muttered gruffly as he undid two more buttons and filled his palm with the sweet, firm round of her bottom.

"It's…a…oh…" She bit her lip and cried out as he tunneled his hand under the elastic of her high-cut panties and found the heat of her. He ran a finger along the damp cleft between her thighs as she expelled a serrated, "sun…dress."

"This…dress—" he hardly recognized his voice as he worked to free another button "—is comin' off."

Her hands raked through his hair, guiding his head to the breast he had half-bared, then moved to the buttons herself to undo them to her waist with shaking fingers.

With effort, he flattened his palms against the screen door and stiff-armed, pushed away. He wanted to see her. He wanted to see the damage he'd done to her lips that were swollen and wet and open for him. He wanted to see the sexual haze in her eyes as she let her head loll against the screen and watched him with anticipation and an impatience that made his mouth go dry.

He wanted to see those beautiful breasts, exposed to the moonlight where her dress fell open to her waist and the thin cotton straps slipped off her shoulders. She looked ravaged and willing and so ripe he groaned with the rush of desire that knotted in his groin.

"You are so unbelievably beautiful," he murmured and looked his fill. She wasn't wearing a bra. She hadn't worn anything but those thin, lacy panties that, even now, drove him crazy just thinking about sliding them down her hips.

Her breasts were pale and round, the weight of them heavy and firm. Her aureoles were a dark, dusky brown, her nipples delicate little velvet peaks.

"Touch me."

Those two whispered words damn near drove him over the edge. He reached out, traced a finger around an erect nipple and felt a tremor eddy through her.

"Like this?"

She closed her eyes, moaned softly when he rolled her nipple between his finger and his thumb.

"Tell me what else you want," he demanded, even as he reached up under her skirt and drew her panties down her legs.

She clutched his shoulders to keep from falling. "Your mouth. I want your mouth."

He dragged her against him then bent her over his arm and lowered his mouth to her breast. Nothing tasted like her. Nothing. He'd never forgotten the feel of her in his mouth, didn't know how he'd lived this long without grazing his teeth along the silk and honey of her skin. Without the salvation that he'd never known he'd been seeking as he suckled and licked and feasted on the heat her answering hunger ignited.

He had planned to seduce her slowly. He had planned to lay her down and love her in the comfort of her bed. He hadn't planned to take her against the wall with the finesse of a water buffalo. But she did things to his plans. Things he didn't seem to have any control over.

Before he knew it, he was reaching for his belt buckle. With his mouth at her throat, he somehow managed to get it open and his zipper down. "My pocket," he said on a guttural growl, surprised that he even had the presence of mind to think about her protection.

He didn't want to use a condom. He didn't want anything between them but skin and heat. But he'd conditioned himself long ago to take care of business and he wasn't going to let his guard down now.

Between the two of them, they managed to get him suited up before he burst with the need to be inside her. He lifted her in his arms, pressed her back against the screen door and with his hands under her bottom, urged her legs around his hips.

"Open your eyes," he commanded and guided himself to the sweet, wet opening that invited him with the sensuous buck of her hips. "I want to see your eyes when I come inside you."

"Hurry," she demanded and when she was looking deep into his eyes, he drove into her.

She drew in a sharp breath; he lost his completely. She was so tight, so sweetly swollen as she took him in—all of him—and held him deep.

He felt something give at her back, heard the muffled rip of the screen ripping and shifted their weight until her back was pressed against the clapboard siding. With his hands on her hips and her eyes locked on his, he moved inside her. Slowly at first because the pleasure was so sharp and so pure he was afraid it would be all over before he'd had his fill of her. He wanted it to last. This deep, drugging sensation of drowning in her, this union of body that veered dangerously close to body and soul.

"Cutter," she whispered his name on a gasping little hitch and knotted her hands in his hair. "Cutter. Please. Oh, please, please—"

He slanted his mouth over hers, swallowing her plea, giving her what they both wanted. With a hard, driving rhythm, he pumped into her body. Clutching her hips to draw her closer, he deepened the contact, extended the pleasure that built and swelled with each deep stroke, with each silken glide.

"Come with me," he demanded, slamming into her. "Come. With. Me."

He felt her peak, and he was gone. His release ripped through him like a lightning strike—all fire and flash and an electric pleasure so fiercely intense that it hurled him over the edge and into free fall. He was lost somewhere in oblivion, riding on the rich, wild aftershocks as she clenched like a velvet fist around him, cried out, and with a shattered sob, flew over the top with him.

Heart hammering, head spinning, he held her hard against him, sweat slicked, artlessly wasted and hung to lucidity by a thin thread of conscious thought that kept him on his feet. He wasn't sure how long he stood there, buried inside her, flattening her against the wall, keeping them both from falling. He was drained, depleted, yet he felt stronger and more centered than he'd felt in years. Maybe six years.

The thought finally sobered him. He was putting way too much importance to something that was merely a hot bout of mind-blowing sex.

Yet when he roused himself enough to lift his head from her neck and look at her face, it wasn't just the sex that he thought about. It was the look of her. Kitten soft and totally vulnerable. Her eyes were closed, her hair falling across her face where his hands—or had it been her hands—had tangled.

With one arm banded around her waist and still buried inside her, he brushed the hair from her eyes. She made a soft sound…of exhaustion, or satisfaction, or discomfort, or maybe all three…and opened her eyes.

"Hi," he said, and touching his lips to the corner of her mouth, fully expected her to call him everything but a child of God for using her so roughly.

A crooked little smile tilted one corner of her mouth before her head fell forward against his shoulder. "Hi? That's the best you can do?"

He chuckled and hugged her hard, amazed at the depth of her giving. "I believe I just *did* the best I

CINDY GERARD   111

can do. And considering I'm still on my feet, I don't think I'd be complaining if I were you—although, Lord, Peg, I didn't mean to be so rough with you.''

"No complaints.'' She raised her head, smiling now, like a very contented, very sexy cat. "But just once Cutter—just once I'd like this to happen in a bed.''

He started getting hard again at the memories that marched front and center. Back then he'd made love to her in the grass, in the back of his truck, on a blanket beneath the stars—but never in a bed.

"Invite me in,'' he whispered, nuzzling his nose against hers, then kissing her eyelids that had fallen closed yet again. "I'll make it up to you.''

She looped her arms over his shoulders and snuggled close. "You're assuming that one of us is still physically able to climb the stairs.''

"Baby...I'd crawl if I had to, to get in your bed.''

He felt her smile against his throat. "There's something very appealing about that picture.''

"You want an appealing picture?'' He caressed her cheek with his palm, arrested by the look of her—all lush and languid and thoroughly loved. "You ought to be standing where I am.''

"There you go again—making an assumption that I can stand.'' She yawned hugely. "I don't think I could get my legs under me if my life depended on it.''

"You don't need to stand...or walk...or crawl. Just hold on.''

Her eyes flew open. She gasped then laughed and tightened her hold when he started moving and jug-

gling and balancing on one foot then the other.
"What…are you doing?"

"Getting out of these boots and pants."

She shrieked and wrapped her arms tighter around
his neck when he almost dropped her. "Wouldn't it
be easier to just put me down?"

He grunted as he finally managed to toe off both
boots and shuck his jeans and shorts. "Easier, maybe.
But not nearly as much fun. Besides. I don't want to
put you down. Can you get the door? My hands seem
to be…full." Of her. Of her smooth bare bottom and
her slim, sexy weight.

She reached behind them, managed to get both the
screen door—which looked like it had been rammed
by a very mad bull—and the front door open. She
laughed again when he stubbed his toe on a bootjack
just inside the door and swore roundly.

"You think that's funny, huh?" He nuzzled the
silky spot just beneath her ear as he climbed the stairs,
her arms still looped around his neck and her legs
still wrapped around his waist.

"I was laughing *with* you."

When he reached her room, he dumped her uncer-
emoniously in the middle of her bed. "Let's see if
you find this funny." He flicked on a bedside lamp
and sat down beside her.

Watching her face, he combed his hands through
the long tangle of her hair. She reached for him,
started unbuttoning his shirt.

"You are so beautiful."

She actually blushed. Color spread downward to
paint everything from her cheeks to her pretty breasts

with a soft, rosy flush. "You're kind of pretty yourself," she said.

He found her sudden shyness endearing. Just like he found her body irresistible.

"Bronc riders aren't pretty," he insisted, cupping one of those beautiful breasts in his palm. He stroked a thumbnail over her nipple, watched it pearl.

She covered his hand with hers, pressing it deeper against her. "Handsome, then?"

"I can live with that." His smile faded when she looked up at him through eyes that had grown slumberous and dark.

He shrugged out of his shirt. "Your turn," he said and went to work on getting her the rest of the way out of her dress.

When she was finally lying there, completely naked, openly vulnerable, he laid a hand over her abdomen. She moved her hips, ever so slightly. He watched, fascinated as gooseflesh broke out across her skin.

"Cold?"

Eyes on his, she shook her head. "I am so *not* cold."

Her stomach muscles clenched beneath his palm and he moved his hand lower, pressing the heel against her pubic bone. "And soft. You are so, so soft."

She reached for him. "And you are so, so hard. Again," she added with a smile that was both seductive and shy.

"And well, we *are* in a bed," he put in philosophically as he stretched out beside her.

"Hmm. There is that." She turned on her side, ran her hand along his shoulder, down his chest and lower, slinging her long, silky leg over his hip. "And then there's this." She caressed him with her soft hand until he thought he'd die from the pleasure.

"Only one problem that I can see," she murmured, nibbling little kisses along his throat.

He gasped, then groaned through clenched teeth. "Problem?"

"The big guy is underdressed for the occasion."

"Wha? Oh, damn." He drew in a resigned breath, settled himself and grinned at her. "Don't go 'way."

Peg wasn't going anywhere. She'd made herself that promise. She wasn't going to the past and she wasn't going to the future. She was going to stay mired right here in the moment, with this beautiful man who even now pressed her into the bed with a hot, hard, claim of a kiss before he rose, gloriously aroused and unashamedly naked.

"I'll be right back," he promised and headed down the stairs.

But as she lay in the dark, listened to his footsteps on the stairs, to the front door creak open then shut, the past intruded whether she wanted it to or not. Through her open bedroom window, she heard him swear softly and pictured him walking barefoot and bare naked across the gravel. She listened to the sound of his truck door open, then close. Only when she didn't hear the sound of an engine firing, did she let out the breath she'd been holding and believe him.

He *was* coming back. He wasn't leaving. At least not right away.

And because she felt too much relief, she reminded herself what this was all about. This was about sex. It was about pleasure. It was about a temporary relief from a loneliness that had settled marrow deep.

None of it was about love.

The hot tears she blinked back when he walked back into the room, dropped his duffel on the floor and a stack of condoms on the nightstand, had nothing to do with love.

The way his eyes looked deep and long into hers when he entered her, moved inside her...nothing to do with love. The careful way he held her through the night, drawing her back against him when she made the slightest move to condition herself to distance...not one single thing to do with love.

And it wasn't love, deep and true, helpless and hopeless, that made her rise at dawn and, wrapped in his shirt, sit in the rocker in the corner of the room and memorize the way he looked, asleep in her bed.

Seven

Cutter was used to waking up to the smell of stale motel rooms and open boxes of leftover pizza. So he figured he must have been dreaming because what he smelled when he woke to daylight and a soft breeze whispering across his bare back was the farthest thing from stale. He burrowed deeper into the pillow, smelled clean, line-dried sheets, a hint of roses, and, could it be? He rolled to his back, sniffed the air and sighed in contentment. Freshly baked cookies.

With a stretch as huge as his satisfaction, he opened his eyes, squinted at the sunlight and got hard, thinking about the night he'd spent in Peg's bed. A bed he could happily spend the next five to seven hundred years in with her.

The thought sobered him like a bucket of cold water.

He was in some kind of trouble, here. He scrubbed a hand over his stubbled jaw, then craned his neck around to the nightstand where a scattering of destroyed foil packets obscured his view of the clock. He lifted his head, let it drop again. Eight-fifteen. He should be on the road. Hell, he should have beat it out of here last night.

But last night he hadn't been able to get enough of her. He ran his hand along the length of an erection that said he still hadn't gotten his fill.

Yeah, Reno. You're in double big trouble.

With a grim set of his mouth, he pried himself out of her bed, snagged his jeans from the floor where he'd dropped them and dragged them on. Carefully zipping to half-mast, he looked for his shirt, gave up when he couldn't find it and barefoot, followed his nose down the stairs.

He'd say good morning. He'd say thanks. Then he'd say goodbye. Before things got too sticky. Before he got too comfortable. Before either of them got to thinking that what was happening between them was something worth thinking about for the long haul. Cutter didn't do long haul. Not when it came to relationships. Not even when it came to Peg.

So, yeah. It was best to be moving on. But then he stepped into her kitchen. And then he spotted his shirt.

His mouth went dry; his jeans became instantly, unbearably tight. And that's when he decided he wasn't going anywhere. Not just yet anyway.

She was making cookies, all right. In her bare feet, with her long smooth legs peeking out beneath the tails of his shirt that hung on her like a tent. The burgundy plaid had never looked so good.

She stood with her back to him, the radio playing softly. She was moving her hips to the music, humming prettily and scooping cookie dough onto a baking sheet that sat on the kitchen counter. He glanced at the oven. The dial was set at 375 degrees. He figured he'd just spiked up to about 950.

She'd piled her hair on top of her head in a loose, untidy little knot that left her neck bare—except for the stray tendrils trailing like silky fringe at her nape and at her temples and when she turned, drifted over her left eye.

"Good morning," she said when she saw him. There were questions in her eyes, but she quickly shielded them and turned back to her cookie dough.

"Good Lord," he managed to say in a fractured croak that had her turning back to face him. "You look…edible."

She smiled, a kind of surprised, mouthwatering, sexy little pleased-with-herself smile when her gaze dropped from his face to the solid ridge pushing against his half-done fly.

"And you look…happy to see me."

He couldn't even be embarrassed, or apologetic. He was too stunned. Too full of feelings he didn't want to analyze, too aroused to consider anything but how he was going to get her out of his shirt. His shirt, that she was barely wearing with both the top and the bottom three buttons undone.

"Did I wake you?" She looked suddenly shy again when he leaned a bare shoulder against the doorjamb and tucked his hands under his armpits to keep from reaching for her. He wanted to look a little longer before he ravaged her.

"I smelled the cookies."

"I just took a batch out of the oven. Sugar cookies," she added, wiping her hands on a towel then slinging it over her shoulder. "You like them?"

He liked damn near everything about this moment. The look of her. The fact that her eyes danced with an edgy expectancy that said she hadn't quite had her fill of him, either.

He pushed away from the door, and because he couldn't not, he walked toward her. "Well, I guess the proof is in the tasting."

"It hit me this morning after I'd done chores and showered that I'd promised to bake cookies for the Friends of the Library bake sale this afternoon." She turned to scoop another ball of dough onto her spoon, then roll it in a sugar and cinnamon mix before smashing it with a fork on a cookie sheet. "I'm making a double batch so help yourself."

"Oh..." He lowered his mouth to her nape and wrapped his arms around her waist. "I intend to."

When he pulled her against him, she leaned back into him, sighed dreamily. He spread his hands wide over her abdomen, loving the feel of nothing but warm flesh and smooth skin beneath his shirt. Not even panties, he realized with a low groan as her little bottom snuggled right up and nestled against his arousal.

"Well, I'd say *you're* fully rested," she observed dryly.

It was one of the things he liked about her most. Her sense of humor. Her willingness to go with the moment, give in to the feeling and to what made them both feel good.

"I don't know…" He nuzzled a spot that was soft as silk just beneath her ear, found a warm, heavy breast and squeezed gently. "You worked me over pretty good last night."

"What's the matter, cowboy? Was the ride a little too rough for you?"

He smiled against her neck. She smelled of soap from her shower and cookie dough and just about the best of everything he'd ever smelled. "The *ride,* was just the way I like it. But I need to refuel."

She turned in his arms. Kissed him softly. "How's that for starters?"

"Umm. Not bad. You taste like your cookies."

"Couldn't resist. They're best when they're warm out of the oven."

"Wrong." He backed her up to the counter, then lifted her and sat her on its cold surface. "They're best before they're baked. I'm a sucker for cookie dough."

She looped her arms over his shoulders, grinned. "I always figured you for a dough boy."

He laughed. "Such a smart mouth." He kissed her, slow and deep and thorough. "Such a *sweet* mouth." Then he kissed her again. "Only one thing I can think of that might be sweeter."

He dipped a finger in the cookie dough. Brought it to his mouth. "Good." He licked his finger thoroughly, all the while watching her face. "But no comparison to you. Hmm. Let's try this.'' Again, he dipped a finger in the dough, then rolled it in the sugar and cinnamon mix.

''Getting closer,'' he said and made a production of licking his finger clean, while her face flamed and his other hand stroked her bare leg, his thumb riding tantalizingly close to the juncture where hip met thigh. ''But I think we can do better.''

''Better? Um…Cutter…'' His name feathered out on a shaky little breath when he went to work on the buttons of his shirt and laid it open.

He loved the view, loved more, the idea of pleasuring her.

''Cutter…what are you…doing?''

''Shh. I'm not done with my taste test yet.'' Making a place for himself between her thighs, he dipped his finger back into the dough.

''Taste test?'' she managed to say on a husky little whisper when he very slowly and very methodically frosted her right nipple with the sugar and butter-rich dough.

''Taste test.'' He heard the gruffness in his voice, wasn't able to take his eyes off the pretty mess he'd just made of her. ''To see…Lord, that's pretty.'' He stopped, drew in a shuddering breath, bent to her breast and gave it one more try. ''To see if I…can come up with…a combination that's even…sweeter.

''Be still,'' he commanded softly when she squirmed.

She caught her breath on a fractured little hitch as his tongue swirled over her nipple.

''Cutter—''

122   TAMING THE OUTLAW

"Shh." Snagging her wrists, he pulled them above her head and pinned them against the cupboard door. "I need to concentrate. And I need to be…thorough. Very," he murmured as he nibbled and licked his way around her nipple, "very…thorough."

"Cutter." It was more groan than protest this time, a beautifully embarrassed and achingly aroused sound that urged him on to more.

"Gettin' there." Watching his handiwork, he frosted her left nipple. He licked her once, wetting her skin, went back for more when she arched and pressed against him. But he wasn't finished with her yet. He was so not finished.

Pinching a finger full of the sugar and cinnamon mix, he sprinkled it over her breast that was wet from his mouth, sticky with dough until she sparkled and quivered in the sunlight slicing in through the window.

Her eyes were slumberous and dark when she tugged her hands free, cupped his face in her palms and pressed her breast to his mouth.

It was all he could do to keep from devouring her, had to make himself be gentle as he nipped and sucked and tasted the sweetest, softest heat, until tasting wasn't enough for either of them.

She was whimpering when he lifted her off the counter, carried her upstairs and laid her back in bed. And pleasured her some more.

With his hands. With his mouth. With everything he had in him, he made love to her. She cried his name, clutched at his shoulders when he lifted her hips, tilted her to his mouth and finally tasted the very sweetest part of her.

Only after he'd tumbled her over that edge where she was destroyed by sensation, dazed by spent desire, did he move back up her body, sheath himself in her clenching warmth and find his own shattering release.

And only when she lay sleeping beside him, and he watched her—couldn't stop watching her—did he realize that this time, this time, it was going to be hard as hell to walk away.

Careful, so as not to wake her, he made himself ease out of her bed. He stood there beside it for a very long time, watching her breathe, watching the soft flutter of her closed eyelids as she drifted on a dream and snuggled deeper into the tangled sheets.

On a long, deep breath, he turned, headed for the shower. It took a long time to wash away her scent. Longer still to rinse away the wanting to crawl right back in her bed and lose himself in all that womanly heat. And not just for the sex—although the sex with Peg was like nothing he'd ever experienced before or since that long lost summer. He just wanted to hold her. Be something more to her, more for her. Something, he admitted, as he toweled himself dry, he wasn't cut out to be.

When he'd pulled on clean jeans and wandered into little Shelby's bedroom, it took longer still to drag his gaze away from the pictures on the dresser. There must have been a dozen of them of Peg and that little girl with the flyaway blond hair and eyes the same color blue that he faced every morning in the mirror.

Panic. Elation. Anger. Denial. Every emotion that had been prowling around the edge of his consciousness since the first time he'd seen that precious child jockeyed for shape and form and substance. He resisted everything but the denial. Assured himself he had no ownership here. Even less long-term interest.

And yet he stood there, seeing too much, maybe even wanting too much before he finally turned, packed his bag and carried it out to his truck.

When Peg woke up and didn't see his duffel on the floor by the bed, she knew Cutter was gone. It didn't stop her from walking straight to the window, brushing back the curtain and confirming it. Her truck was there—Krystal and Sam had made good on their promise to deliver it. When she didn't see Cutter's truck in the driveway, however, she reminded herself she was not going to let it hurt this time.

She dressed mechanically, combed her hair and finished baking her cookies. Then she walked out to the barn, hating herself for the weakness that had tears stinging behind her eyes. And for the knee-jerk urge she'd been fighting to track him down and beg him to stay.

She wouldn't do that to him.

More important, she wouldn't do it to herself.

She walked over to Jackpot's stall, absently stroked his hip and wished Shelby was home. She missed her. She missed her baby girl. The ache in her chest and the tears that started leaking down her cheeks had everything to do with missing her—nothing to do with Cutter.

"Rascal, come here boy," she whispered, then indulged herself in something she hadn't let herself do since the first time Cutter Reno had turned his back and walked away. She sat down in the middle of the barn floor, wrapped her arms around Rascal's warm, silky neck and bawled like a baby.

She'd pretty much gotten it out of her system when she heard a vehicle pull into the driveway. She wiped her eyes, got up to look out the door and felt her heart skip. *Cutter.*

He was back. Too much hope. Too much joy. It danced through her blood and made her realize how truly pathetic she was. And how angry she was with herself for letting him get to her this way.

She quickly combed her fingers through her hair then hunted around in the tack room for the pair of sunglasses that she knew—she *prayed*—she'd left there yesterday.

She was not a woman who cried willingly or often. And when she did, the aftermath was not pretty. Her eyes, when she'd met them in the cloudy tack room mirror, were puffy and red—so was her nose—not to mention her lips. They'd swelled up like they'd been bee-stung.

"Peg? Peg, where are you?"

She sent a thank-you skyward when she found the glasses, slipped them on and on a bracing breath, answered him.

"In the barn."

Then she made herself busy in Jackpot's stall with a currycomb. She was brushing like a machine when she heard him slip inside.

"Hey," he said when he spotted her.

"Hey yourself," she tossed brightly over her shoulder. Too brightly evidently, because he was suddenly behind her. He touched a hand to her hair.

"What's up?"

It wasn't a casual what's up. It was tender and concerned, like he could tell she'd been crying when that was the last thing she wanted him to see. Just like the last thing she wanted was Cutter being tender and concerned. Aloof and casual, she could handle. But not this.

"Just thought I'd give the outlaw here a little TLC," she hedged then prayed he'd walk away so she wouldn't have to face him.

"Peg?" he said after a long moment.

"Know what?" she said breezily and shouldered past him with her head down so he couldn't see her puffy face. "I forgot about running those cookies into town. I'd better get them in there before—"

His hand on her arm stopped her. He turned her slowly toward him.

She kept her head down, fussed with the bristles in the brush. She wouldn't look at him. She couldn't.

"You thought I'd left." His words were dead cold, dead serious, dead-on.

"No—no…I—" She tried to turn away again. Again, he stopped her.

"Yes. You did. You thought I'd left. I wouldn't do that to you. I wouldn't leave, Peg—not without saying goodbye."

She stood statue still, her head down, her lower lip starting to tremble as he spread his broad palm along her jaw, edged his thumb under her chin and forced her to lift her head and look at him.

He searched her face for the longest time before he reached over, tugged off her glasses.

"Damn," he said. "I'm sorry."

She finally found her voice and surprised them both with the bite in it. "You think this is about you?" She laughed, then touched trembling fingers to her lips, pinched her eyes shut. "Shelby," she insisted. "I just got to missing Shelby. So stop looking at me like that. Stop looking at me period. I'm a mess."

"You're a beautiful mess." He pulled her into his arms.

Because it felt so good there, she pushed away. "You can lighten up on the sweet talk, Cutter. You got what you came for. And so did I. I got exactly what I wanted from you."

Bitterness. She heard it, hated it but she let it hang there, along with the lie, until the heat and the hardness in his voice fractured the silence.

"And what was that, Peg? What exactly was it that we both wanted?"

"Sex," she said bluntly. "That's all this is about. And it was great." And she wasn't. She wasn't great. She was miserable and she could hardly believe she'd said those words, that she'd lied right through them, even thrown in a convincingly tired breath for good measure.

But hey, never let it be said that she wasn't a fast learner. Cutter had just taught her another good, hard lesson. He still had way too much ability to hurt her. She wasn't going to let it happen. Not again.

"Look, Cutter. Don't turn this into something it's not, okay? We both knew going into this that you were just passing some time. Well, it worked out fine because so was I."

His eyes turned hard as he watched her. "Passing time."

"What else would you call it?" Misery built to anger as he stood there and acted as if she was the one breaking the rules when it was his game they were playing. It had always been his game. The one that ended with him riding off into the sunset and left her standing here missing him.

Well, not this time. She couldn't stop herself from baiting him. "Or was I reading you wrong? Do you have plans to stay this time?"

He had nothing, *nothing,* to say to that. And because he'd been offered the chance and rejected it, it hurt that much more.

"You don't have a very high opinion of me, do you?"

"I don't have an opinion, either way," she said, as the fight slowly fizzled out of her.

"Oh, I think you do. I want to hear it."

"No," she said quietly, "you don't. Look, I've got to deliver those cookies." She pushed past him and all but ran toward the house.

Cutter stood there and watched her go.

Sex. It was all about sex, she said. He worked his jaw, feeling hollow and angry and for one of the few times in his life, hating—really hating—the man he'd become. The man who had made her cry and then run away.

She wanted him gone. She'd made that clear enough. Fine. He'd leave. It was probably for the best anyway since it didn't appear as if there was going to be a good end to this conversation no matter what kind of a spin he put on it. Besides, he didn't feel much like spinning. And she was right. He was leaving. He always left.

Face grim, he walked back to his truck, reached over the tailgate and snagged the roll of screen that he'd driven into town and picked up at the hardware store. He'd managed to round up a wire cutter, rip the old screen off the door and cut the new to size by the time Peg headed out the front door, a plastic container of cookies in hand.

She stopped short when she saw him there, rolling up the old screen that they'd destroyed last night.

"Oh. Oh," she said again and he saw in her face that she'd just put it together that when he'd left, it had been to go to town to buy the replacement screen. When her face flushed red, he knew she was also thinking about how it had gotten broken.

"You…you don't have to do that."

"I broke it. I'll fix it." He started tacking it in place.

She didn't seem to know where to look, or what to do.

He knew, though. He knew just what to do and if his heart slammed a little with the decision, he'd just have to deal with it.

"I'll be gone when you get back from town," he said and turned to face her. "Being that I got what I came for and all."

Her gaze shot to his. He watched as his angry words settled, as she digested. And he waited. He waited for her to say she was sorry, she hadn't meant what she'd said earlier, she didn't want him to go.

"Oh... Well, then..."

He stared at her very beautiful but very bruised expression and felt like he'd just beat up a kitten.

Dammit. It didn't have to be this way. He could have stayed. He'd wanted to stay. At least he'd wanted to stay a little while longer. But he knew when he wasn't wanted—just like he knew when it was time to hit the road.

"You take care of yourself, Peg."

"Sure," she said quickly. Just like she smiled too quickly. Those big brown eyes searched his face one last time, before she looked away. "Sure, Cutter. I always do."

Then she walked to her truck and tore out of the driveway.

And for the first time in his life, Cutter knew what it felt like to be on the receiving end of a bad good-bye.

He couldn't say he liked it much.

Couldn't say he liked it much at all.

But it was for the best. He didn't want to stick around until Shelby came home next week. He didn't want to see those blue eyes smile at him and face a truth he wasn't yet ready to accept let alone deal with.

He couldn't say why he headed in the direction he did when he left Peg and Sundown behind. He should have gone south. There was big money and important points to be won as he chased another invitation to the NFR. But after eight hours on the road, he pulled up in front of a little tan house flanked by blooming red rosebushes and tidy green shrubs.

It looked homey and well loved. A nice place to live. Good, Cutter thought, as he walked up the steps and lifted the shiny brass knocker. He was happy for the woman who opened the door with a dish towel in her hand.

She blinked once then started crying through her smile. "Cutter."

He slipped off his hat. "Hi, Mom."

For the second time that day, he felt guilt over this new talent he seemed to have developed for making strong women cry.

It was late that night and he wasn't yet ready to bed down in the room she always kept ready for him. Just in case he came home.

She was so glad he'd come home that it made him feel guiltier still for the months that had passed since he'd last made the trip. And then it had made him feel good when she'd happily fussed over cooking him supper and he'd made her laugh over his stories of the rodeo.

They'd moved into the living room, him nursing a beer that she also kept stocked just in case, and her with a cup of tea. He could see that she was tired. Just like he knew she would never admit it. Because he was finally home, she wanted every minute she could squeeze out of their time together.

"What was it like? Having him use you and then leave you?"

Anna Reno looked stricken at first, both in surprise and at the bluntness of his question. He felt the shock of it, too, hadn't known it had been prowling away back there, looking for an opening to break out.

"I'm sorry, Mom." Pain mixed with the shock on her face. "I shouldn't have asked. It's none of my business."

But then, in that way she had of reaching for strength and understanding his need, she squared her shoulders and she told him. She told him exactly what it was like.

"It was like being nothing. Less than nothing. Like constantly being asked if I wanted to go for a ride and then being left waiting by the side of a long, dusty road with no water, no direction and the sun going down."

He sat beside her on the sofa, propped his elbows on his wide spread knees and stared at his clasped hands. Is that how Peg felt? When he left her—is that how she felt?

"It took a while," she continued softly. "To understand that the fault was his, not mine."

His head snapped up. He frowned at this woman who deserved so much more than she'd ever gotten out of life and out of the man who had made a vow to love and to cherish. "Yours? You actually thought it was *your* fault that he was such a bastard?"

She touched his face, love shining in her eyes over his defense of her. "I thought it was my fault that I couldn't make him a better man. I'd had hopes, Cutter. I...I loved him once. It's not easy for a woman to give up on love. But there came a time when I finally realized it wasn't him I was trying to hold on to as much as it was the idea of loving him."

Restless, he stood, walked to the window. "I hate him for what he was. And for what he wasn't."

She was quiet for so long that his heart had firmly set up residence in his throat and his hands had grown damp and clammy.

"And you're afraid you'll turn out just like him."

He clenched his fists, closed his eyes, stunned yet not surprised by her perception. Somehow, it made it harder to say the words—to break the news that he had turned into one more disappointment for her. "I already have."

He pulled out the picture then. The one he'd lifted from Shelby's room. The one he'd stuffed in his shirt pocket and hadn't let himself look at but had committed to memory.

He turned back to his mother, handed her the photograph, watched her face as she studied it, ran her thumb across it lovingly.

"So," she said, tears swimming in her eyes when she looked up at him, "you're a daddy."

"Yeah." He felt his heart thud with the weight of admitting it for the first time out loud. "I'm a daddy."

The emotions he'd refused to deal with since first laying eyes on Shelby hit him with a sucker punch that nearly sent him to his knees.

"I don't want to be like him," he said and heard the anger and the anguish and, oh, God, felt the biting sting of tears.

He dragged a hand roughly through his hair. "I've

already lost her first five years, Mom. Five years,'' he ground out, defeated and angered by the truth it. ''Why? Because I am like him...and her mother knows it.''

He sank back down on the sofa, buried his head in his hands. He resisted for only a moment before he let her pull him into her arms, let himself cling to her, let himself feel the anger and the shame and the guilt of it all. And the fear. Oh, yeah. There was fear. A child. He had a child. A beautiful, bright, thriving child who didn't even know she had a daddy.

He didn't know the first thing about responsibility. Didn't know the first thing about what it took to grow up, to own up, to be what she needed him to be.

''Tell me about her,'' his mother said gently. She brushed the hair back from his forehead, wiped her thumb across tears that wet his cheeks. ''Tell me about both of them. Then tell me what you're going to do.''

Eight

Peg and Shelby and Peg's mom were sitting on the swing on Jack and Kay's front porch. It was Friday afternoon. Peg had hopped in her truck and raced over from the feed store the minute Kay had called to tell her they were home from San Diego.

"I can't get over how big you've gotten in just two weeks. I swear, you've grown an inch!" Peg exclaimed, as she hugged Shelby then set her back so she could look at her. They'd had supper, the dishes were done and she still couldn't stop looking at her—or touching her. "Must be all that California sunshine."

"Or the gallons of ice cream Grampa Jack couldn't resist buying for her," Kay offered dryly, smiling, too, as she watched her daughter and wondered at the subtle change in her.

"How're things with you, honey?" Kay asked casually.

Peg looked at her mom. At her pretty brown hair that she wore short and sleek, at her trim figure and golden tan. At her brown eyes that were watchful and all seeing and she knew she'd done a lousy job concealing her feelings.

Peg looked away, grabbed Shelby and hugged her until she giggled. "I'm great now that my baby's back home. Did you miss me? Even a little? Or were you having too much fun?"

"I didn't get homesick, did I, Gramma? Not once."

"Well, I got homesick for you." Shelby gave Peg a hug that told her everything she wanted to know. She'd missed her mom.

"What do you say we head for home and get you unpacked? Rascal and Bea have been watching for you for a week now."

"Okay." Shelby bounced out of the swing to go look for her duffel. "Grampa Jack and Gramma Kay are sure gonna miss me, though, aren't you?"

Kay grinned then tried to look properly disappointed. "Absolutely, sweetheart. But we'll be okay."

The screen door slammed behind Shelby. "She's quite the girl," Kay said as she watched her go.

Peg smiled, nodded, then clasping her hands together around her updrawn knees, stared down the quiet street.

"What's wrong, Peggy?" Kay asked, her eyes gentle, her intuition, as always, tuned in to Peg's feelings.

"Nothing. Nothing's wrong." Peg glanced at her

mother then away. "I...I just didn't realize how much I was going to miss her, is all." She smiled for good measure.

Kay watched in supportive silence, waited for Peg to give it up.

"Oh, Mom," she said at last and lowered her forehead to her knees. She would not cry for him. Not again. She shot off the swing, leaned against a porch post. "I'm so stupid."

"You are a lot of things, honey, but stupid isn't one of them."

"If I'm so smart, then why did I spend last weekend with Cutter?"

Kay was quiet for a long time before Peg heard her rise, poke her head in the door and ask Jack to keep Shelby occupied for a few minutes. Then she walked back to her daughter and without a shred of judgment in her eyes, encouraged her to tell her all about it.

It was a full week later and after ten o'clock on Monday night when Peg's phone rang. She'd already turned in but she wasn't asleep. She'd been trying to lose herself in a mystery and wasn't having a bit of luck doing it.

She picked up her portable phone from her nightstand midway through the second ring—figuring it was Krystal or her mom or something equally routine.

"Hello."

"Hey."

Everything inside of her went still at that one word uttered in Cutter's whiskey-and-honey voice. She'd have recognized it in her sleep. She'd dreamed of it too many nights to make her sane.

"Joe?" she said, because she was miserable enough and felt just ornery enough for paybacks. "Is that you, honey?"

"Cute, Peg. Real cute."

She could hear the fatigue in his voice along with a clatter of background noise as neither of them said anything at all. She clung to the receiver and told herself to hang up. To do the smart thing and just hang up the phone. Instead she pulled her knees to her chest and clung to the silence, her heart pounding, her eyes closed tightly shut.

"So," he said finally, "how's it going?"

"Fine," she squeaked out, cleared her throat and tried again, her mind racing. Why had he called? Why hadn't he called sooner? Why was she stupid enough to care? "It's going fine. You?" she asked because she couldn't stand the disquieting silence that followed but couldn't make herself break the connection.

He sighed heavily. She heard laughter in the background along with a shout for more beer while country music blared loud and strong. He was in a bar, partying, no doubt, and with his judgment clouded by beer, must have decided it was a good idea to call her.

Yet he didn't sound as if he'd been drinking when he asked, "Shelby get back from California?"

Her heart picked up another beat. She willed it to settle down. "Yeah. Last week."

"Had a good time, did she?"

Another double beat. It was not guilt. She would

not feel guilty that he was asking about his daughter
and didn't even know it. "Yeah. She had a great time.
Cutter, what's on your mind?"

He was quiet for so long she wanted to jump
through the line and drag a response out of him. Then
it was fear, not indecision that sent her pulse rate
rocketing.

"Is something wrong? Oh, Cutter…are you hurt?"

"No," he said, finally. "Nothing's wrong. And I'm
fine. Won the go-round tonight," he said, almost distractedly, as if he just wanted to fill space, to keep
her on the line.

"Well…congratula—"

"—I want to see you again," he cut in—more demand than statement. More growl than request. When
she just sat there, speechless, he tried again. Softer
this time. "Please, Peg. I want to see you."

She couldn't find her voice. Wasn't altogether sure
that was a bad thing because she honestly didn't know
what she'd say if he pressed her. Oh, she knew what
she should say. Forget it. I don't want to be your port
in a storm. I don't want to be your flavor of the
month.

*I don't want you to hurt me again and tempt me to
tell you about Shelby.*

Before she could say no, don't come, don't call,
his voice came back on the line. "Just…just think
about it, okay?"

Thinking was what got her into trouble. Thinking
maybe she meant more to him than a good time.
Thinking that maybe, just maybe there was something

more on his mind than another round of hot sex and a fast goodbye.

"Look, Peg…I've got to go. The guys dragged me down to this bar to celebrate and they're getting restless. I'll call you. Tomorrow. I'll call you tomorrow night, okay?"

The line went dead. And she was left alone in her bed to wonder at the absurdness of her hope and at the resilience of her heart that might not survive another hit from Cutter Reno.

She had her answer the next night. She could live through darn near anything. But it got harder. It got so much harder because as it turned out, he did the one thing she knew she could count on. He didn't call.

Foolishly she'd waited by the phone until almost eleven o'clock. Calling herself ten times an idiot, she'd finally gone to bed—disgusted with herself for wanting him to call, angry with him for planting the seed that he'd really intended to follow up on his promise in the first place.

Nothing had changed. Nothing would change. It was just like she'd told her mom. She didn't understand this attraction she felt for him. She didn't understand this need. It didn't make any sense. It could come to no good. Not for her. Not for Shelby. Cutter was all for Cutter. His wants. His needs. His broncs.

Anger finally gave way to grim acceptance. She drifted off to sleep after midnight, promising herself she was never going to fall for the promises in his voice or in his eyes or in the way he made love to her. Not ever again.

She wasn't sure how long she'd slept when something woke her. She was instantly awake, painfully alert, her heart pounding, her eyes wide as she looked at the clock on her nightstand. Two-fifteen.

"You should lock your door."

She bolted up in bed, the scream dying on her throat when she recognized the shadow in her bedroom doorway. Tall, lean and broad shouldered, he walked on silent steps across the room, turned on her bedside light.

She dragged the hair out of her eyes, hiked herself up in bed. He looked exhausted. Like he'd driven through hell to get here. To get to her. She shook her head. Begged him with her eyes not to make her want him this way again. Not to make her hope—even as she felt his arms wrap around her, draw her close and kiss her like he'd die if he didn't taste her now. Right now.

His eyes were closed, his fingers shaking when he pulled away, pressed his forehead to hers and touched a hand to her hair.

"You...you said you'd call," she whispered inanely.

"I lied."

"You...you shouldn't be here." Already his hands were roaming her back, bunching up her sleep shirt, tugging it over her head.

"I couldn't stay away."

She caught her breath on a gasp as he bent his dark head to her breast, nuzzled, adored, indulged.

"Shelby—" she protested as he laid her down then

went to work on the snaps on his shirt.

"—Is sound asleep."

She whimpered when his bare chest pressed against her breasts. Naked heat, muscled and lean. "She...she can't find you here...in my bed."

"She won't. She won't. Shush. Shush now, let me love you. I can't...I can't stand not loving you."

"Cutter," she groaned his name, dug her fingers into his shoulders as he entered her, long and strong and deep. "Oh, Lord, Cutter."

He hiked himself up on his elbows, pushed the hair away from her face. Cupping her head in his big hands, he watched her face as he penetrated and withdrew, penetrated and withdrew. His eyes were dark, his soul bled through them. "It's not just sex. It's *never* been just sex," he ground out even as he shuddered and fought to hold back his release. "Say it. Tell me it's not just sex."

She was drowning in sensation, lost in a love so strong she couldn't, no matter how vulnerable it made her, continue with the lie. "It's not just sex. It was never just sex. Never."

She clenched her teeth to keep from crying out as he swept her over the edge and held her there—suspended somewhere between sweet heaven and fiery hell. And then she was flying, soaring like a rocket, flaming like a star as he took her to that place where nothing but him mattered, nothing but them made sense. And nothing but reason—lost the moment he'd crushed his mouth over hers—could have kept her from taking the ride.

* * *

Cutter winced, shifted painfully to a sitting position and blinked at the blue eyes peeking through his driver's-side pickup window. Shelby grinned when he glared at her, pressed her nose against the glass and a little *tap, tap, tap* with her finger that must have woke him up.

He dragged his hands through his hair, rolled down his window and shook himself awake.

"Who are you?"

He got the giggle he wanted. "I'm Shelby, silly."

"Shelby Silly. I don't know any Shelby Silly. I know a Shelby Lynn Lathrop, but she wears this pair of scruffy old red boots. You got any red boots?"

She clamped on to the door handle and grunting comically with the effort, lifted one tiny foot shod in bruised red leather and a broken-down heel up to window level. "See?"

"Well, I'll be darned. It is you."

"Yup. It's me," she said all cheerful and bright and happy to have that cleared up. "Hi."

He smiled. "Hi yourself, blondie," he said forgetting about his kinks and his aches and his pains and the fact that he'd crawled out of her mother's warm bed at 4:00 a.m. to insure that Shelby didn't find him there and get the wrong idea. Like maybe he was there because he belonged there, or because he planned on staying.

He hadn't planned on going to her bed. Honest to God, he hadn't. But he'd pulled up, dead tired and dead wrong about what he was going to do. It hadn't been just her bed that had beckoned him. It had been everything. The little house that she'd made a home.

The arms that felt sheltering and warm. The child that she had yet to tell him was his.

He didn't blame her. Couldn't blame her. What reason had he ever given her for thinking she could trust him to be anything but heartache—for her or for Shelby.

He still hadn't sorted everything out in his head. That's why he was here now—he needed to do some sorting with Peg. Some sorting and some talking and some explaining—only he wasn't yet sure he had the guts to do it.

"My mom's still sleepin'," his daughter said, still hanging on the door, her little feet perched on his running board. "Boy, is she gonna be surprised when she sees you."

"Good surprised or bad surprised?" he asked, playing devil's advocate.

"Oh, good," she said with utter confidence. "I told her just last week that I wished you'd come see us again and now you're here. How 'bout that?"

Yeah, he thought, watching this child that was his and falling a little deeper into something he suspected ran very close to love, *how 'bout that.*

"How about we surprise her," he suggested, "and make her breakfast?"

"Cool." Shelby jumped down from the truck. "But we got to hurry 'cause she's gotta go to work and I gotta go to Krystal's. Did you know I start school next week?"

"High school?" he teased as he shouldered open the door and crawled out of the cab.

"Kindergarten, silly, 'cause, duh, I'm only five."

"Oh, yeah? How long have you been five?"

Even before she told him, he knew it had been since April. April 2 to be exact, she informed him.

"That means I missed your birthday." Like he'd missed all of her birthdays, a thought he tried not to dwell on because it made this hollow little ache settle and weigh like lead.

"Do you usually get presents on your birthday?"

No dummy, this child. She regarded him with curious and hopeful eyes. "Lots."

"Well, then you probably don't need this one." He reached behind the seat and pulled out a brightly wrapped package.

"Wow!" She plopped down right there in the driveway and tore into it.

He hunkered down beside her, watching with a guarded hopefulness that told him her reaction meant more to him than he'd ever thought.

"Oh, wow!" she cried again when she pulled out a pair of shiny new red boots. "Just what I always wanted! Oh, thank you, Cutter!" Then she launched herself into his arms, complete joy, absolute trust.

He was still recovering from the jolt of it, from the unequaled pleasure of his daughter's warm little body snuggled against his, when she ran off like a shot, forgetting all about him as she sailed into the house and clamored up the stairs.

"Mom! Mom!" she cried. He winced, knowing Peg was going to have a rude awakening after a very short night of sleep. "Guess who's here! And look what he brought me."

He'd missed so much, he thought, as he walked

slowly up the front porch steps. Rascal came trotting out of the barn, his tail sailing high in a friendly wag.

"Hey, boy." He bent down to scratch him behind the ears. Then he sat down on the steps and waited to be invited inside.

The sound of Peg stirring, of Shelby's giggles had him looking toward the distance for absolution and the capability to not be angry with Peg.

He'd missed so much.

He'd missed so damn much.

Peg sat at her little kitchen table while Shelby tromped around in her new red boots and Cutter—who seemed to fill her tiny kitchen with his presence—stood at the stove flipping eggs.

How had this happened? She lowered her head to her hands. How had she let this happen again?

It's not just sex. It's never been just sex. Say it. Say it isn't just sex.

Cutter's raggedly whispered words played back in her mind as she ate the eggs he'd cooked for her and drank the juice he'd poured. She watched as he slipped another piece of bread into the toaster because Shelby had wanted one.

What did he want?

The look on his face as he sat down across from her and watched her over his coffee mug told her he wasn't sure himself—that he was a long way from figuring out the answer to that question.

"I have to go to work," she said, refusing to let something that looked desperately like need in him, achingly like vulnerability, convince her there was anything but convenience behind his unexpected visit.

"I know," he said.

"And I get to go to Krystal's," Shelby piped up as she munched on her toast. "What do you get to do today, Cutter?"

He looked at Peg over the steam rising from his coffee cup. "I guess I get to wait for you."

Do I get to wait for you, his eyes asked. *Can* I wait for you?

Peg rose, set her plate and glass in the sink. "Feel free to use the shower and catch up on your sleep…on the sofa," she added. She did not want to work all day with a picture of him sleeping in her bed hovering in her mind. "You must have driven half the night to get here."

"Yeah," he said. "I did." Unspoken was the, *"And I'd do it again."*

That was the part she didn't want to think about because that was the part that made her do stupid things—like think he might be thinking about staying.

It's not just the sex.

"Come on, Shell," she said, hearing the desperation in her voice and not caring. "We need to get rockin' or I'm going to be late. Run upstairs and get your backpack, okay, baby?"

"I'll take care of the dishes," Cutter said and she just stopped for a moment and stared.

"What are you doing here, Cutter?" she whispered when Shelby had scooted out of earshot.

"I just wanted to see you." He reached for her, pulled her slowly into his arms.

She pressed her palms against his chest, met his eyes. "And?"

He let her go. Turned and stared out the window. After a long moment he faced her again, leaned a hip against the counter. "And I wanted to talk."

Her eyes asked what she couldn't put into words.

"About us."

She was scared stiff by the probing look on his face, unable to stall the panic that his next words confirmed she had every reason to feel.

"You. Me. And Shelby."

She could hardly breathe and yet she'd known, somehow she'd known that Shelby was the reason he'd come back.

"She's mine, Peg," he said and she watched, stunned, as he worked his jaw and fought to hang on to his emotions. "I know she's mine."

She closed her eyes, resigned and somehow relieved before the panic kicked in double-time. "She doesn't know. She doesn't know. Cutter, please... please—"

"—Don't hurt her? You think I'd *hurt* her?" His voice rose to a dark demand.

She warned him with a look to keep it down.

"You think I'd intentionally hurt her?"

She walked to the table, gripped the back of a chair with unsteady hands. "Every time you drove away."

Her quiet certainty hardened his gaze and set his jaw working.

"Every time you drove away because your rodeo was more important to you than she was—you would hurt her."

She stared at her hands, at the knuckles that had gone white, then made herself look at him. She was determined to make him understand—even at the cost of her pride.

"I can take it. Watching you leave. Knowing you won't be back until and unless it suits you. I can take it, Cutter. She couldn't. She...just couldn't."

He crossed his arms over his chest, looking angry and belligerent and guilty. Mostly guilty. It was the guilt—an admission that she was right, that he would always leave—that helped drive her point home.

"Please—if you care about her..." She watched the tension that set his mouth in a grim, hard line and stayed the course. "If you care about her, be gone when we get home tonight."

Aching—heart deep, soul deep—she turned and walked away, disappointed but not surprised when he didn't try to stop her.

It was two weeks before Peg heard from him again. As luck would have it, Shelby was on a sleepover with her friend, Marty, when she came home from work on a Friday night and found him—just sitting there in his truck in her driveway.

When she thought her legs wouldn't buckle, she got out of her truck. Her arms loaded with a sack of groceries, she walked over to where he was parked. Rascal was sitting on the seat in the cab with him, looking happy and smug and totally in love.

Which she wasn't. Even though she ached just looking at him. Even though she'd wanted and wished and prayed that he was someone she could count on, that maybe he could change. But two weeks was a long time and it told a pretty clear story. Six years told an even bigger one.

When she'd asked him to leave, he'd done it. No argument. No plea for understanding. No phone calls asking for the same. If he really wanted her, if he really wanted Shelby, he would fight for them.

Instead he'd just walked away.

And now he was back. She didn't know what it meant. Couldn't let herself wonder—couldn't stop herself from asking.

She gathered herself, felt the fatigue and the wanting and refused to give in to either. "Why do you keep doing this, Cutter? Why do you keep showing up here?"

He opened the truck door, got out and relieved her of the groceries. "Because I can't stay away," he said bluntly and headed for her porch.

Peg stared after him, then getting ahold of her senses, coaxed Rascal out of Cutter's truck and shut the door behind him.

"What does that mean?" she demanded, catching up to him as he pulled open her front door.

"Don't you ever lock anything?" he snarled, his anger flashing, white-hot and without warning. "Don't you know that anybody could just waltz into your house, take what they want? Hurt you if they wanted? Hurt Shelby? What's wrong with you?"

"Hold it!" she snapped, an outrage as alive as she'd ever felt boiling up and taking over. "Just—"

"—And why don't you have a decent watchdog?" he demanded, rounding on her. He gestured toward the door in disgust. "He doesn't even bark, for Pete's sake. What good is he?"

She flashed on a picture of Rascal gazing adoringly at Cutter, his big hand stroking his coat with affection.

"What right do you have?" she shot back and grabbed at the sack of groceries. "What right do you have…showing up here whenever the spirit moves you and laying into me about how I manage my life? Give me those." She reached for the sack but he refused to let go. "And go away. Just go away!"

"You don't want me to go." His blue eyes were stormy and more than a little steamed. "You just don't know what to do with me now that I'm here."

She tugged, angry beyond belief because he was right. He was so right. The sack ripped. Oranges and apples and little boxes of juice and tins of vegetables flew all over the floor.

"Dammit! And damn you."

"You don't think I am? You don't think that I'm as damned as the devil?" he roared and bent down beside her where she'd dropped to hands and knees to frantically gather her spilled fruit and get away from him. Just get away from him.

"I can't stop thinking about you," he confessed, sounding tortured and confused and beside himself with frustration. "I can't stop thinking about Shelby."

She steeled herself against the torment in his voice. "Yeah, well, that's your problem, not mine."

She cried out when he grabbed her arms and pulled her up against him. "I'm making it your problem."

He hated this, she realized. Hated that he hadn't

been able to stay away. That he'd come all this way and she was fighting him instead of falling into his arms.

She hated it, too. Hated the hurt he caused every time he left her. Hated the guilt she felt over keeping him from Shelby—hated more that every time he left, he proved that she'd been right to do it.

She started crying then. And she hated herself for that, too. But once she started, she couldn't stop. All the anger, all the indecision, all the years of guilt and loneliness and sense of betrayal burst from somewhere deep inside where she'd hidden the pain, denied its existence.

"Aw, damn. Peg. Don't. Sweetheart, don't. Please don't cry."

He cradled her against him, there on his knees on the floor, with apples and oranges tumbling around them.

"It hurts, Cutter," she cried, clinging to him. "It hurts. I can't do this. Don't. Don't do this to me anymore."

The breath that soughed out was unsteady and deep. "I don't want to hurt you. I never wanted to hurt you. Never."

He stood then, picked her up with him and carried her to the sofa where he sat down. Then he held her. Just held her while she clung to him and cursed him and cried.

Nine

Making love didn't solve anything. But it felt good when they'd both felt so bad. So they ended up in her bed again, where they could lose themselves in pleasure and forget the pain they caused each other.

And somehow, in the midnight hour, with both of them stripped to the skin and vulnerable, it made it easier for Cutter to say those things to her. Those things he needed to say.

He knew she was awake. As he lay there in the dark with her warm and snug and silent beside him, he knew. Just like he knew it was up to him to either begin or end this thing between them. *Begin or end.* He was starting to think that the "b" word wasn't as threatening as it had once been. Yeah, it still scared him, but it had a better ring to it lately. A better ring than the other one. The one that was so short and so concise and so unalterably final. The one he'd been so good at using all his life.

"I'm sorry," he said, stroking a hand along her bare hip. "I'm sorry I wasn't there for you."

He was glad she didn't pretend that she didn't know what he was talking about. Doubly glad that she, too, was ready to talk.

"I didn't give you a chance to be there for me."

She began to pull away, to distance herself, but he held her fast, held her close.

"Why didn't you tell me?" The anger was there, he couldn't stop it even though he knew she didn't deserve it. "No. Wait. That wasn't fair. I know why. Because I was a self-centered, selfish, sonofabitch who didn't have a clue. That's more than enough reason."

He felt her relax then turn into him. "Jack wanted to go get you."

He snorted, squeezed her hip. "I'll just bet he did. Why didn't you let him?"

She thought about it for a moment as she trailed her fingers up and down the length of his arm. "Because I didn't see any point in both of us being miserable."

Yeah. He would have been miserable. Miserable to live with, miserable to stomach. And he would have made her miserable, too.

He turned to his side, reversing their positions, pressing her to her back. Propping himself up on an elbow, he watched his hand as he spread his fingers wide over her flat abdomen. He could span the breadth of her from hip point to hip point with his fingers. Suddenly he wanted to know everything that he'd been so sure he'd never want to know. Suddenly he wished he could have seen her, her belly swollen with the child he had put there.

"Was it hard? Were you sick? Was it…did it hurt you a lot?" He leaned down, pressed a kiss to the firm, resilient flesh and silken skin that had harbored their daughter. "You're so small, Peg."

She told him then. With his cheek against her abdomen and her hands threading lightly through his hair, she told him about the morning sickness, about the labor, about the joy of seeing that squished little red face bawling into the world like a summer storm.

He was quiet for a long time, thinking about it. Regretting that he'd missed it. Honestly not knowing what he'd have done if he'd known—and hating himself even more because of his selfishness.

He lifted his head, and she smiled at him. "Do you want to see pictures?" At his horrified look, she laughed. "*Baby* pictures, not delivery pictures. Are you green, Reno?"

He hugged her then kissed her—because of her strong and forgiving heart—and he realized in that moment that his feelings for her ran deep. Deeper than he'd ever let them run before. So deep it scared him. So deep he couldn't talk, couldn't think for the force of them.

"Peg," he said, filled to bursting with words he didn't know how to say. Words that would mean little to her since he hadn't figured out what they meant for either of them. So he kissed her, just kissed her, instead.

She smiled then eased, beautifully naked, out of bed. "I'll be right back," she said and slipped into his shirt.

She came back a few minutes later with a tray of fruit and some granola bars—they'd somehow managed to skip supper—and an armful of photo albums.

Then they sat cross-legged on the bed until three in the morning, and he'd gotten to meet his baby daughter. Grinning and toothless. Drooling and adorable. There were several pictures of her on a springy rocking horse. Even at two, she'd worn her trademark red boots. He smiled over dozens of pictures of her on Bea. Pictures of her in nothing but the bathtub and bubbles.

Did all fathers feel this way? he wondered. Did all fathers feel this pressure near to bursting in their chests as they looked at something they had been a part of making? Something that was someone so special it brought a stinging pressure to the back of his eyes?

"I didn't trust you not to hurt her, Cutter." Her soft confession brought his head up from the images of his daughter. "I'm sorry."

"No. You were right." He didn't like it much but he was solid in the admission. "It was all about me back then. I wasn't man enough. I wasn't good enough. Not for her. Not for you."

Her eyes misted. She looked away.

"I'm not sure I'm man enough yet," he confessed and felt his heart sink when her silence told him that she wasn't sure of him, either.

"I don't lock my doors," she said, her eyes fierce

and true, "but I'd die for her, Cutter. I'd die before I let anyone hurt her. That's why I didn't tell you. That's why I don't know if I ever would have told you."

He understood. He understood perfectly what she was telling him now and couldn't fault her for it. "I won't hurt her. And I won't hurt you. Ever. Not ever again."

She wanted to believe him. Her eyes shimmered with that want. But her heart, battered and bruised from the scars he'd put there, wasn't ready to let her.

"I want to be with her. I won't tell her," he said quickly when panic made her face go pale. "I promise. I won't tell her I'm her daddy. Not until—not unless," he amended, "you say the word. I just want to be with her, Peg. And I want to be with you."

She looked down, gathered the pictures and folded the albums shut. "Rodeo is your life. It's your livelihood."

She didn't have to say the rest of it. He knew the rest of it all too well. Rodeo was also the road. Long, empty stretches of it. And rodeo had taken its toll on more relationships than he could count.

Not for the first time, he felt stirrings of doubt. He didn't know the first thing about building a relationship that didn't start with the intent to leave already factored in. But he did know one thing. He didn't want to leave this woman. When he was with her, he never wanted to leave—yet somehow, the reality was that he always did. And he didn't know what to do about that, either.

"Just...just don't say no, okay? Peg..." He shifted,

set the albums aside and took her hands in his. "Just...can we give it a try? Can we see if we can make something work between us?"

"Sure, Cutter," she said after a long moment but her sad smile told him she gave it no hope at all. Because she knew him. She knew what he was and she knew that leaving was what he did best.

He kissed her then, tried to tell her without words that he didn't want to stand on that track record any longer. Wasn't near as proud of it as he'd once been—but neither was he sure what lay beneath this new leaf he wanted to turn over.

As he laid her down and loved her, he tried to forget that he was his father's son. He tried to lose himself in her warmth and forget that he was the farthest thing from a sure thing that a man could ever be.

And as she took him in, became one with him, he realized that for the first time in his life—for Peg, for Shelby, maybe even for himself—he wanted to be more. He wanted to be the surest, steadiest thing in their lives. He wanted it bad. As bad as he'd ever wanted anything.

Even knowing that, even as he raced over the edge where there was nothing but him, nothing but her, nothing that mattered but them, he'd be damned if he knew if he had it in him not to let them all down.

"Cutter!" Shelby cried at ten o'clock that morning when Peg had collected her from Marty's and brought her home. "Mom, Cutter's here!" she said through a bubbly laugh when Peg pulled her truck into the driveway and parked it by Cutter's.

Peg had barely cut the engine when Shelby had her seat belt unfastened and was scrambling out the door.

Cutter unfolded himself from the porch steps where he'd been sitting—all grins and good looks—as Shelby ran up the steps and launched herself into his arms like a rocket.

"Whoa, there, cowgirl." He laughed as he hugged her.

Peg felt the hot sting of love behind her eyes and met Cutter's gaze over their daughter's flyaway blond hair. Her smile was bittersweet as Shelby chattered and quizzed and snatched his hat off his head and set it on her own.

"When did you get here? How long are you stayin'? Did you win last week? Krystal and Sam get the PRCA News so they tell me how you did but they didn't get it yet this week so I've been wonderin' and wonderin'."

"You ever hear about the cat that got done in by curiosity?" Peg asked her daughter as she joined them on the porch.

Cutter just laughed when Shelby launched into another round of questions. "How 'bout I fill you in while we ride?"

"Really? We're goin' ridin'?" She looked from Cutter to Peg, excitement glittering in her eyes. "Are we goin' ridin'?"

"Mighty fine day," Cutter said, his eyes dancing. "Be a shame to waste it."

So, of course, they went riding. And it only made

sense to pack a picnic lunch—because Shelby hadn't been on a picnic in *forever*. For that matter, neither had Peg and she'd found herself humming as she'd prepared sandwiches, feeling happier and more hopeful than she'd ever remembered feeling. Maybe she was deluding herself but for this one day, she didn't care.

Was it so crazy to think he meant what he said? That he wanted to be with them? That he wanted to make something work between them? She didn't have any answers. She didn't think he did, either.

And later that night, after Shelby had taken her bath then conned Cutter into reading her a story, was it insane to think something had already started to happen?

He hadn't heard her walk quietly down the stairs after her shower. He wasn't aware that she stood there in the soft light watching them snuggle together on one end of the sofa. The book was forgotten; Shelby was curled up on Cutter's lap, sleeping the sleep of angels.

Peg's chest filled with a hope she'd refused to let herself feel as she watched his dark head bent over their child. The hands that held Shelby were so big yet infinitely gentle as he held her close. Tears misted Peg's eyes as he drew a deep breath and pressed a kiss to the top of Shelby's head.

"Sweet little girl," he murmured into the silk of her baby-fine hair. "You just may make a daddy out of me yet."

That's you, Shell, she thought, awash with a swell

of love and longing for both of them. *A low-down, sneaky little daddy maker.*

She swallowed the lump in her throat and walked toward them, these two people who meant the world to her. "You want me to take her?" she asked quietly.

He didn't respond for a long moment. When he raised his head and met her gaze, she could see she wasn't the only one moved by the moment. "She's so beautiful, Peg. It's still hard to believe I could have had a part in making someone this unbelievably perfect."

His voice was gruff with emotion, his eyes suspiciously bright.

If she hadn't already been in love with him, she would have fallen right then. Alley cat or not. This rodeo-loving, woman-leaving man was so deep under her skin she could no longer draw a breath that wasn't filled with him. Couldn't form a thought that didn't start with him. End with him.

"She loves you." It was an offering, a gift she could no longer withhold although he would have to have been blind to have missed it.

"I don't ever want to make her sorry for that. I don't ever want to make *you* sorry for that."

It was bittersweet, this love she felt. He was trying so hard to be what he needed to be for both her and Shelby. And yet it was so apparent that he still had his own doubts about fulfilling that need. And because he had doubts, she understood that her own reservations were still founded in reality.

"Then don't," she said simply. "Don't ever make us sorry."

The blue eyes that met hers were as tortured as they were beautiful. She felt his panic, recognized his fear. This talk of trying, this whisper of the promise of commitment was uncertain ground for him. He was as afraid that he'd fail as she was.

Why, Cutter? What are you so afraid of? And why hadn't she yet worked up the courage to ask him?

It wasn't just rodeo. It was more. There was an emptiness in his eyes as he rose and carried Shelby up to bed. There was a desperation in his kisses when he took her to bed later and loved her.

Just like there was a sadness in her heart when he woke her at midnight to kiss her goodbye and promise to call her the very first chance he got.

For a long time after she heard his engine fire and the crunch of gravel beneath his tires had faded to a memory, she lay awake in her bed that felt empty and cold. And she tried not to think how like a ghost he was. How he'd come to her so often in the night, and leave her the same way. Needy and wanting, restless and seeking.

What are you missing, Cutter? What do you need that we can't give you? And what's it going to take to finally make you stay?

"Are you sure you know what you're doing?"

The chill in the air had as much to do with the edge in Krystal's voice as it did with the cool evening temperature. Even this early in September, nighttime brought the reminder that winter was only a couple of months away.

"As sure as I am of anything these days," Peg said and double-checked the contents of the suitcase she was in the process of packing.

"I just don't want you setting yourself up for a big fall."

Peg refolded one of Shelby's sweaters, laid it in the suitcase and sat down on her bed beside Krystal. "This is *so not* the song you were singing in July."

Krystal tucked her leg up under her and fussed with the throw pillow she hugged to her lap. "Yeah, well, maybe I was singing the wrong tune."

"And maybe you should stop worrying that what you said had any influence on the decisions I've made about Cutter."

"Thanks. I think," Krystal said with a crooked grin. "Nice to know you value my sage advice."

"What I value is your friendship. What I value is knowing that you care."

"I just don't want to see you hurt. Not by him. Not again."

"She loves him, Kris," Peg said simply. "Shelby loves him to death. And he loves her. I can't keep them apart. Not anymore."

It had been three weeks since they'd seen Cutter. He'd called almost every night. To talk to her. To talk to Shelby. And last night, he'd called begging them to come to him.

"Say yes, Peg. Please. Say you'll come. You and Shelby. We'll make it a long weekend. I've got to see you but this is a key competition. I can't miss it.

Please. You'll love Dallas." He'd gotten a little quiet then before he'd finally confessed, "I want you to see me ride."

From that point on she'd been lost. He'd already arranged for airfare. All they had to do was get to Missoula to catch the flight. Krystal was here to take them.

"And what about you?" Krystal asked, bringing Peg back to the moment.

"*What* about me?" Peg rose and zipped up her luggage.

"Shelby loves him—do you love him, too?"

Her hands stilled momentarily then got busy lifting the bag from the bed to the floor. "Are you going to refuse to drive us to the airport if I say I do?"

Krystal rose, too. She came around the bed and hugged her. "Nope. I'm just gonna say take care, kid. Don't let him hurt you."

Peg hugged her back. "Well, if he does, it'll be my fault, won't it, for letting myself get in this deep." She pulled back, gave Krystal a bracing smile. "Now come on. I've got a plane ride to get keyed up for. Lord, I hope it's not one of those puddle jumpers that's held together with rubber bands and duct tape. I do not want to embarrass myself by getting sick."

"You won't get sick. You'll enjoy every minute of it. So will Shell."

And they did—puddle jumper and all. They switched planes at Denver and made the rest of the trip on a jumbo jet that was almost as fascinating as the look on the face of the cowboy that met them in the Dallas terminal.

"Cutter!" Shelby cried when she spotted him, all lean smiling male and more handsome than any man had a right to be.

"Hey, blondie." She launched herself at him. "How's my best girl?" Laughing, he scooped her up in his arms and hugged her against him—all the while telling Peg with a long, hungry look how much he wanted to find someplace where he could show her how much he'd missed her.

"And how's my other best girl?" he asked as he walked toward her.

"Fine," Peg managed to say as he set Shelby on the floor beside him.

He held on to Shelby's hand, never taking his gaze off Peg. "I'm gonna kiss your momma now, Shell. That all right with you?"

"Sure, sure, sure. Just get it over with so we can get to the rodeo."

They were both smiling as he moved in close, touched his other hand to her hair. "Hi," he whispered.

"Hi," she whispered back just before he found her mouth with his and gave her the softest, sweetest, most lonesome kiss she'd ever tasted in her life.

"I've missed you." He pressed his forehead to hers, sighed in contentment.

She felt young and foolish and in love and not caring that anybody within eyeshot knew it. Anybody within eyeshot happened to take the shape of a bow-legged cowboy with a toothy grin and an Adam's apple that bobbed nervously while his face turned three shades of red.

"Ah, Cutter..." The Oklahoma drawl was as warm as sunshine on a cloudless day. "We got to be gittin' if we're gonna make the first go-round. Ma'am," he added and flushed red all over again when Peg smiled at him over Cutter's shoulder.

"That would be Burt," Cutter said, drawing reluctantly away and tucking Peg under his shoulder. "Burt Winslow, Peg Lathrop. And this cute little blonde with the bright red boots is Shelby Lynn."

"Hey, Burt," Peg said.

"You're a bronc rider," Shelby said, clearly in heaven, surrounded by cowboys. "I saw your picture in the PRCA News."

"Hey, there, little Shelby." Burt's Adam's apple bounced with every word he said. "You ready to see the rodeo?"

"You bet!"

"Why don't you go on ahead with Shelby and see about catching the luggage, Burt." Cutter handed him the claim stubs Peg had dug out of her purse. "We'll catch up in a sec.

"She's okay with him," Cutter assured Peg when she cast a worried look toward her daughter, who happily trotted along toward the luggage carousel, hand in hand with the lanky cowboy. "But I'm not gonna be okay until I do this."

He pulled her with him to a corner on the other side of the flight monitors and backed her up against the wall. "Sorry. This is as much privacy as I can arrange—at the moment." And then he kissed her— like she'd been aching to be kissed, like he couldn't draw another breath until he got it out of his system, or got the taste of her into his.

"We're...creating...a...spectacle," she said between the assault of his hungry mouth and busy, busy hands.

"Don't care," he growled as he dived in for another kiss that turned her knees to noodles, sent her heart rate into overdrive and her mind into a mush that didn't care anymore, either.

They were both breathing hard by the time he lifted his head then buried his face in her neck and held her close against him. For the longest time, he said nothing. He just held her—as if she were the anchor holding him steady in a storm determined to sweep him out to sea.

"Cutter..." She touched a hand to his hair. "Are you okay?"

"I am now." He pulled away, smiled at her. "Come on. Let's go see if Shelby's talked Burt's leg off yet."

Peg hadn't seen Cutter ride since that summer six years ago. Sure, you couldn't live in Montana without catching the occasional rodeo on TNN or ESPN or sometimes even some local TV coverage. And yes, she'd caught snippets of his competitions a time or two on TV. Shelby, after all, was a rodeo junkie. But Peg had watched with reluctance and she'd watched with resentment and it hadn't been the same.

In person, from the VIP seats he'd arranged for her and Shelby alongside Tracy Grover, Wreck Grover's wife, and their little girl, Katie, Peg saw Cutter and the sport he loved in a whole new light.

He was something to watch, this defending National Finals Saddle Bronc Champion. He was something to be reckoned with. And above all else, he was a man in his element. A man who knew his job and loved it.

The crowd loved him, too. So did the media—and the women. For three nights running, the hordes of lush and lively buckle bunnies who vied for his attention had sent the occasional daggered look her way.

"Whoa-ho," Tracy said with a huge grin as she dug into a tub of popcorn. "If looks could kill, you'd have been dead ten times tonight alone."

Tracy was a petite little blonde, a veteran of the rodeo life and as much a fan as Shelby. Peg had liked her immediately when they'd met the day before yesterday. It had also helped that Katie and Shelby had become fast friends.

"You sure those looks aren't directed *your* way? Wreck's a fine-looking man."

"Oh, no, sweetie. Those women know not to go poaching anywhere near my territory. I may be little, but I fight dirty. Besides, Wreck's as true-blue as they come. He also knows I'd kill him real slow and painful-like if he ever so much as poked a toe outside his own pasture.

"Nope. Those daggers are definitely meant for you. Cutter's little bunnies aren't used to getting cut out of the herd and, honey, since he made that trip back to Sundown in July, he hasn't given a one of 'em the time of day. Not that he ever really had much time for them anyway. Katie June, you put that down. How many times have I told you that you do *not* pick up anything from the floor? You don't know where the boots have been that might have stepped on it first.''

Peg grinned then returned the glare of a redheaded woman in paint-tight jeans and knee-high boots. ''If he didn't date them then why are they so upset with me?''

''Well…until you, they at least thought there was reason to hope. Cutter's never brought anyone with him before,'' she added on a meaningful note. ''Not even once.''

The crowd cheered as the team-roping competition heated up. Peg leaned back in the seat, thinking about what Tracy had said, surprised by the information. ''How long have you and Wreck been together?''

Tracy laughed. ''Since dirt. We grew up—both of us—as rodeo brats. My daddy has a stock contracting company and Wreck's daddy was a pickup man for years. Guess you could say rodeo's in our blood.''

''Where's home?''

''When we get there, it's Stephensville.''

''Texas?'' Shelby piped up, suddenly tuning into the conversation. ''That's where Ty's from.''

''Yep. We're neighbors.''

''Ty's the best,'' Shelby said adoringly, '''Course, that's only after Cutter. And Wreck and Burt.''

''Girl's got good taste—and tact, too,'' Tracy added with a grin.

''Not to mention that she's fickle,'' Peg added

with a smile. "Ty Murray was the man until Cutter showed up."

"How about you," Tracy added pointedly. "You fickle, too?"

Before Peg could figure out how to respond to that, Tracy rushed on. "None of my business, I know. But the thing is, we go way back—Cutter and Wreck and me. I just…I just want you to know that you're capable of hurting him. And sweet as you are—if you hurt him, I'd have to hurt you. I just wanted you to know that." Then Tracy smiled and hugged her.

Peg was dumbfounded. *She* was capable of hurting *him?*

It was a thought that had never, not in a million years, crossed her mind. She was stunned by the prospect. Shaken by the possibility. And by the time the night's events were over and they were working their way through the crowd to head back to their hotel room, she was starting to wonder if all this time—all this time—the heart that was most vulnerable had actually been his.

Ten

It was late. They were back at the hotel and it was their last night together before Peg and Shelby caught their flight to Missoula in the morning and Cutter headed for Houston. Shelby was bunking with Katie in Tracy and Wreck's set of rooms—the girls had wanted to giggle away their final night together. Peg, just out of the shower and wearing a short midnight-blue gown, was standing in the doorway of the adjoining rooms Cutter had booked for them when he walked out of his own shower, a towel slung low around his hips.

He was so deep in thought as he sat down on the edge of the bed that he wasn't aware she was watching him. His hair was damp; his face was hard. Her heart hurt at the look of him—at both the beauty and the pain. The beauty was there, always there, for anyone to see. The pain, he rarely let anyone witness. The pain, she realized now, was something she had never recognized in him.

She recognized it now. It wasn't physical, although his body had taken a beating. It always took a beating in competition, even a successful competition as this one had been.

As he lay back on the bed, stared at the ceiling, she saw the weight of another pain so clearly now and wondered why she hadn't seen it sooner. Because he'd never let her—because even *he* hadn't come to terms with the source of it. But most of all, because she'd been so afraid of the pain he was going to cause her and Shelby, she'd never realized he was struggling with his own.

Earlier tonight, Tracy had made her stop and think and realize that there was more than rodeo that made Cutter run.

You have the capability to hurt him.

Like he was hurting now.

Lonely.

The man was lonely and he didn't know what to do about it. She wasn't sure that she did, either, but as she walked into his bedroom, she was determined to figure out a way.

He turned his head when he heard her, hid his feelings behind a brilliant smile.

"Scoot up," she said. "And roll over. I'll give you a back rub you'll never forget."

"A man would have to be crazy to turn down an offer like that." He ditched the towel and did as she asked, until he was lying spread-eagle on his stomach.

She was the one who was crazy. Crazy in love. And crazy because it had taken her this long to figure out that he was in love with her, too. Just as she'd figured out that he was scared with the knowledge of it. Didn't trust himself to know how to handle it.

He groaned into the bedspread when she straddled his hips and started working on the knotted muscles in his neck. "You have magic hands. Why don't I turn over so you can work your magic on some other very needy parts of my poor beat-up body."

It would be so easy to go there with him. To lose herself in his arms, to let him show her what he couldn't find the courage to tell her. She leaned down, pressed a kiss between his shoulder blades. "Later, cowboy. Right now, just lie still and let me do this for you."

His skin was hot, his muscles tense. "Don't move. I'll be right back."

She slid off the bed, walked into her room. When she found her body lotion, she returned and settled over his hips again.

"Whoa—that's cold." He shivered when she squeezed a line of lotion down his back.

"It'll warm up."

"And it smells—cripes, Peg—it smells like flowers. You're gonna have me smelling like a girl."

"Just so you smell like *my* girl."

His snort was muffled in the bedcovers. "Lucky for you, you've got such great hands or I wouldn't put up with your lip—or your lotion."

"Lucky for me," she said on a smile and worked on a stubborn knot under his shoulder blade.

She watched her hands move over his broad back, felt the strength of the muscle beneath his skin, hesitated over a scar here, another one there—reminders of the risk of a sport that claimed many casualties. The physical evidence was obvious. It was the other scars she wanted to find and soothe tonight—the ones that had nothing to do with riding broncs.

He was relaxed now; she could feel the subtle softening of all that firm muscle. His breath had slowed to an even, restful cadence.

"Where's home for you now, Cutter?"

Her question surprised him—it surprised her. She hadn't known that was where she was going to start. It also reminded her just how much about him she didn't know. The sum total of their relationship to date had been a long-lost summer love affair and a handful of days and nights together since July—some of them fighting, most of them making love—and hundreds of long-distance phone calls. Conversation had been limited to Shelby, to rodeo, to the weather, to how much they missed each other. They never talked about the future, never talked about the past. And it was the past that Peg suspected held the key to whatever future they might have.

The way Cutter's muscles momentarily tensed before he made himself relax again said he was more than surprised by her question. He wasn't comfortable with it and the doors it might open.

Finally he moved a shoulder. "There's a motel in Denver that holds the same room for me every time I blow into town. Does that count?"

He tried to make light of it but she knew that light

was a far cry from what he was feeling. *Lonely.* It was in his voice—just as it had been in his eyes before he'd seen her watching him.

He wasn't the only cowboy who carried everything they owned in their rigging bag along with their saddle and a duffel that they threw in the back of their truck. He wasn't the only cowboy who didn't have a home to go back to. But he was *her* cowboy and she needed him to open up to her.

"Have you seen your mom lately?" she asked, slipping off his back and stretching out beside him. She pressed herself against all his hard heat and propping her head on her hand, continued to stroke his back in a slow, circular caress, keeping that all-important connection.

He crossed his arms in front of him then rested his forehead on his stacked hands. "A couple of months ago. She's doing good." He drew in a long breath, let it out. And fell silent.

"I remember her," she said softly. "I always felt bad for her. She seemed so…sad."

His eyes were closed but she saw the muscle in his jaw tighten, felt his body tense as well.

"What happened?" she pressed as she maintained the contact of her hand on his back. "With her and your dad? I don't ever remember seeing him."

Another silence, one she was afraid he'd withdraw into and leave them exactly where they were.

"What happened is that he's a sonofabitch."

That much she'd suspected so it was little more than she'd had before. "Do you ever see him?"

"Nope."

End of discussion. Door closed.

She wanted more but after several tense, silent moments, it became clear she wasn't going to get more. And maybe that was for the best. Maybe it should be up to him now.

"Wanna play a game?"

One corner of his mouth crawled up into a grin that had her smiling in spite of herself. "Thought you'd never ask."

"Not *that* kind of game. Pay attention. What am I spelling?" With the tip of her finger, she drew a letter on his back.

"Sex."

She popped him on the shoulder. "Sex does *not* start with *I*. Now be serious."

"Okay. *I*."

"That was a gimme. Now guess the rest."

With light, deliberate strokes she spelled another word.

"*Love.*" His throat worked as he swallowed. He wasn't smiling anymore.

She spelled yet one more word.

"*You,*" he said on a hoarse whisper and started turning toward her.

"Not yet." She pushed him back to his stomach. "There's more."

"*Home,*" he said when she'd finished.

Her eyes were swimming with tears when he turned to her and repeated the rest of the words she had spelled on his back. "Home is here with me."

Eyes locked on hers, he drew her into his arms and kissed her—like he was coming home, like he was craving home, like he was starting to believe that maybe he had found home for the first time in his life.

The next morning, he put her and Shelby on the plane.

And Peg waited. A full three weeks passed—without a word from him, without a call from him—before she accepted that she'd scared him off. Her talk of love, her talk of home hadn't opened the door to their future. It had slammed it in her face.

She would have hurt for him—if she hadn't been so busy wanting to hate him for the hurt he'd caused Shelby. Wanting to hate him for refusing the love she'd offered because he'd been too much of a coward to accept it.

She loved him. Cutter had been running from those words for three weeks. Running and denying and telling himself he was doing everyone involved a favor by making the break hard and clean.

He'd hit three more rodeos since then. Had cinched his fourth invitation to the National Finals in Vegas in December—even had a good shot at another championship. Seven years ago, when he'd thrown his hat into the ring, he would have been the happiest man on earth if he'd known he would be this successful.

Seven years ago, he'd measured success by day money and points, by hard rides and good times. As little as four months ago he'd used the same yardstick.

Now he didn't know. Now the victories felt hollow. The nights—always long—were haunted. With thoughts of her. Of losing himself in her eyes. Of losing himself in the eyes of his daughter.

She loved him—or thought she did. They both loved him. And that's the part he couldn't handle. That's the part he couldn't trust.

"You know, Reno, that pretty face of yours has gotten as long as the highway between here and Galveston and I, for one, am getting damn sick of lookin' at it."

Cutter glanced across the booth into the scowling face of Tracy Grover. They were at some truck stop on some highway on the way to another rodeo. He didn't remember the name of the place, didn't care. Everything had started to blur since Dallas.

"If you're so tired of looking at it, why did you ask me to breakfast? Never mind. Don't answer that. Where's Wreck and Katie, anyway?"

"Sleepin' in," she said, "and don't change the subject."

"I didn't know there was a subject."

"For a smart man, you sure pull some dumb stunts."

"Eat your breakfast, Trac—it'll give you something to chew on other than me." He shoveled a forkful of scrambled eggs into his mouth and swallowed in stubborn silence.

"Go after her."

He froze, braced the edges of his palms on the booth top, then leaned back and stared out the window where a fleet of semis lined up to fill their tanks.

"You're entitled, Cutter. You're entitled to something good. So is Peg. Now for God's sake, be a man and go after it.''

He whipped his head around, glared at his friend. The compassion in her eyes took the bite out of her words.

''Be a man. Be the man she needs,'' she said, then slipped out of the booth and walked away.

It was close to midnight and three days later when Cutter pulled into Peg's driveway. He cut the engine and sat there. Exhausted. Exhilarated. Scared to death that he'd blow what would undoubtedly be his last chance with her. Even more scared that before he got the chance to tell her what she deserved to hear, she'd tell him to hit the road or go to hell or drop dead. She was more than entitled.

The house was dark. And when he walked up the porch steps to let himself quietly inside, the door that was never locked was locked against him. He pressed his forehead to the frame, closed his eyes and for the first time, considered that there might be no bridges left to burn.

He also considered leaving, saving them both another round of pain.

Be a man. Be the man she needs.

Tracy was right. He owed Peg more than an explanation and he wasn't leaving until he'd at least given her that.

Knowing it would be a waste of time to try the back door—no one could make a statement like Peg—he went right for the side of the house directly below her upstairs bedroom window. It took his pickup and the long ladder that he found in the barn, but he finally managed to reach the window, cut the screen, and with the help of a long-handled screwdriver, ease the window open. His booted foot had just hit the floor when her bedside light flicked on.

He whipped his head around—and drowned in the look of her, soft and sleep tousled, wary and wounded from all the distrust he'd fostered.

"Trust you to miss the point of a locked door."

He watched her face carefully. "I've missed a lot of things since Dallas."

She dragged the hair back from her face with both hands. "If this is another hit and run, Cutter, I'll pass—thanks, anyway."

Bruised. She looked bruised and weary and as distant as the rodeo in Texas that he'd skipped to get here.

"I don't blame you," he said, holding his hat in his hands to keep himself from reaching for her. "I don't blame you for hating me."

She turned her face away, shook her head. "If only it was as simple as that."

She looked so vulnerable—this strong woman who showed no fear. He'd done that to her. He wanted to make it right.

Taking a chance, he crossed the room and sat down on the edge of the bed. She watched him warily as he memorized the cinnamon-brown of her eyes, the chestnut sheen of her hair, the silky skin that still held the hint of a summer tan. He wanted to touch her so badly he ached with it. Wanted to feel her pliant warmth against him, ease them both over the line where there was nothing but ragged heartbeats, blazing body heat and hard, mindless loving.

But he couldn't get by on that alone anymore. She needed more from him. He'd finally realized that he needed more, too.

"When I left Sundown eight years ago," he said carefully, "it was because I wanted to be someone. And I wanted to get away from my mom's sad eyes."

He paused, not looking at her now, but at a frayed tear in the knee of his jeans. "I hate myself for that—for leaving her alone. I hate that I've run from sad eyes ever since."

This was harder than he'd thought. Saying the words. Laying out his failures.

"I wanted to be better than my old man." He shook his head, smiled without humor. "The only part he'd played in my life had been an accident of biology yet I wanted to show *him* what I was made of. That I was worth ten of him."

Another deep breath. He looked toward the window, to the midnight sky, then back at her. "It took you—it took loving you to make me realize I'd turned out just like him. It took Shelby to make me see—really see—how like him I was."

"Cutter—"

"No. Let me get this out. I'm not good with words. Not important words. I love you, Peg. Those are important words. You were entitled to hear them long ago."

It was so easy, and it felt so right to finally say it. And such a relief to stop fighting it, as he'd been fighting it since that summer so long ago.

He loved her. He let himself just slide into the feeling, like slipping into a comfortable pair of boots, or a pair of soft, worn jeans or into her when she was wet and hot and ready for him. Easy. Natural. Right. And suddenly the rest of the words just came to him.

"There is nothing about you that I don't love. I love the way you look, the way you laugh, the way you love—both Shelby and me—with every single part of yourself."

Her eyes were closed now, her head down as she clutched the sheet in her hands.

"I love the way you kiss…the way you look at me when you take me deep inside."

A small sob escaped her and then she was in his arms. He didn't know who moved first, he only knew that he was finally holding her, feeling her heart beat against his, burying his face in the sweet scent of her hair.

"You've made me think about things," he whispered, bracketing her face in his hands so she was forced to look at him, to see him as the man who loved her. "Things like home. I've been afraid of believing in that, too, but I've finally figured it out. You did that. You made me see that home *is* you. It's not a place. It's a feeling. It's a pair of red cowboy boots."

She laughed then and he wiped the tears away from her cheeks with his thumbs. "It's a heart that I trust to be true. I've run away all my life—because I couldn't trust the feeling. Couldn't count on something I'd never had—didn't think I deserved."

"You run away from us again," she said between

tears, "I swear…I swear I'll hunt you down and drag you back here by your pride and joy."

He pressed his forehead to hers then matched the promise in his words with the promise in his eyes. "I'm not running anywhere. Not ever again."

He kissed her then, long and deep and laid her back on the bed.

"You're not him, Cutter." She searched his eyes with love and conviction. "You're not your father. You just thought you should be."

Cupping his face in her hands, she laid his final fear to rest—the one he hadn't known he'd harbored until she voiced it. "And I'm not him, either. I'm not going to leave you. I'm never going to leave you like he did."

She lifted her head, touched her mouth to his. Soft and tender. Wild and sweet. She seduced him with the nip of her teeth, the sweep of her tongue, until they were tearing at his clothes and dragging her nightshirt over her head.

"I love you," he whispered and let her take him. Let her push him to his back beneath her and own him. Let her bend over him, tease him with the sweep of her hair across his skin, tempt him with the brush of her nipple against his open mouth, destroy him with the clench of her silken heat sinking over him, around him.

He gasped, bucked beneath her, dug his hands into her hips as she rode him to an end that left him breathless and spent and in awe of her capacity for giving.

He buried a hand in her hair, fought for air. "I love you."

"I know," she whispered against his shoulder, limp and wasted and secure. "I know."

Epilogue

Two months later, Cutter stood on the winner's platform at Thomas Mac in Las Vegas and accepted his third National Finals Saddle Bronc Championship Award.

Among the seventeen thousand fans that cheered from the stands were Sam and Krystal Perkins, Wreck and Tracy Grover. On one side of Peg were Jack and Kay Lathrop. On the other was Anna Reno, who blinked back happy tears for her son—and for the pure and amazing joy of holding her granddaughter on her lap.

"That's my daddy," Shelby said to anyone who would listen. "And he won that buckle just for me, didn't he, Gramma Anna!"

Later, after the celebration had wound down, Peg watched from the bed as Cutter, stripped down to his bare feet and new jeans, picked up a sleeping Shelby and transferred her from their bed to the one in the second room of their suite.

"She's had quite a day," he said as he stretched out beside her again and crossed his hands behind his head.

"We all have. It's been a wild ten days."

She studied his face, loving the look of him, relaxed and weary and content. "What are you thinking?"

He turned his head, smiled. "I was wondering how you'd feel about being married to a circuit cowboy."

She glanced at the wide gold band on the ring finger of her left hand, the one he'd put there at a small family service Thanksgiving weekend. "Circuit cowboy?"

"I love rodeo, Peg—but I don't need it to be my life anymore. I don't want to be on the road away from you and Shell."

"So you're thinking of pulling out of the big competitions—just work the Montana circuit?"

He shrugged. "Seems like a good compromise. I'd be home all week—rodeo on weekends. The money won't be the same, but I figure if I partner up with Lee Savage like he's suggested—"

"Whoa." Peg came up on an elbow. "Lee wants you to be a partner in his horse business?"

"Well, he's approached me, yeah. Said he'd like to get into bucking stock. Figured I'd be the man to know what to look for."

"But where does the partnership come in? Doesn't that usually require some investment?"

He grinned and rolled to his side, facing her. "You know, there are advantages to living out of a truck or a seedy old motel room for eight years. No mortgage, no utility payments. I've been lucky, Peg. I've put a little money by."

Before she could say anything else, he rose, dug around in his duffel and pulled out some papers. He tossed them on the bed.

She looked at him, looked at them.

"It's the deed to your house—along with twelve hundred acres I was able to convince Homer to part with. I know it's not much—not by Montana standards, mostly scrub grass, but there's water."

She went pale, pressed a hand to her chest. "You bought it? The house? And…twelve hundred acres?"

"What? You don't want it?"

She flew to her knees, threw herself at him, hugged him madly. "I love you."

He held her to his chest and didn't figure on ever letting her go again. This woman—this woman was everything to him and he planned to spend the rest of his life paying her back for what she'd done for him.

She'd made him into a man.

She'd made him a daddy.

She'd brought him home. Home—where he planned to stay for *forever*.

* * * * *

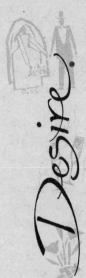

October 2002
TAMING THE OUTLAW
#1465 by Cindy Gerard

Don't miss bestselling author
Cindy Gerard's exciting story about
a sexy cowboy's reunion with his
old flame—and the daughter he
didn't know he had!

November 2002
ALL IN THE GAME
#1471 by Barbara Boswell

In the latest tale by beloved
Desire author Barbara Boswell,
a feisty beauty joins her twin as a
reality game show contestant in an
island paradise...and comes face-to-
face with her teenage crush!

December 2002
A COWBOY & A GENTLEMAN
#1477 by Ann Major

Sparks fly when two fiery Texans are
brought together by matchmaking
relatives, in this dynamic story by
the ever-popular Ann Major.

MAN OF THE MONTH

Some men are made for lovin'—and you're sure to love
these three upcoming men of the month!

Available at your favorite retail outlet.

Silhouette®
Where love comes alive™

$ Saving Money $
Has Never Been
This Easy!

Just fill out and send in this form from any
October, November and December 2002 books
and we will send you a coupon booklet worth a
total savings of $20.00 off future purchases of
Harlequin and Silhouette books in 2003.

Yes! It's that easy!

I accept your incredible offer!
Please send me a coupon booklet:

_____

Name (PLEASE PRINT)

_____

Address   Apt. #

_____

City   State/Prov.   Zip/Postal Code

In a typical month, how many
Harlequin and Silhouette novels do you read?

❏ 0-2   ❏ 3+

097KJKDNC7   097KJKDNDP

Please send this form to:
   In the U.S.: Harlequin Books, P.O. Box 9071, Buffalo, NY 14269-9071
   In Canada: Harlequin Books, P.O. Box 609, Fort Erie, Ontario L2A 5X3

Allow 4-6 weeks for delivery. Limit one coupon booklet per household. Must be
postmarked no later than January 15, 2003.

HARLEQUIN®
Makes any time special ®

Silhouette ®
Where love comes alive ™

COMING NEXT MONTH

#1471 All in the Game—Barbara Boswell
She had come to an island paradise as a reality game show contestant. But
Shannen Cullen hadn't expected to come face-to-face with the man who had
broken her heart nine years ago. Sexy Tynan Howe was back, and wreaking
havoc on Shannen's emotions. She was falling in love with him all over again,
but could she trust him?

#1472 Expecting…and in Danger—Eileen Wilks
Dynasties: The Connellys
They had been lovers—for a night. Now, five months later, Charlotte Masters
was pregnant and on the run. When Rafe Connelly found her, he proposed a
marriage of convenience. Because she was wary of her handsome protector,
she refused, yet nothing could have prepared her for the healing—and
passion—that awaited her in his embrace….

#1473 Delaney's Desert Sheikh—Brenda Jackson
Sheikh Jamal Ari Yasir had come to his friend's cabin for some rest
and relaxation. But his plans were turned upside down when sassy
Delaney Westmoreland arrived. Though they agreed to stay out of each
other's way, they eventually gave in to their undeniable attraction. Yet
when his vacation ended, would Jamal do his duty and marry the woman his
family had chosen, or would he follow his heart?

#1474 Taming the Prince—Elizabeth Bevarly
Crown and Glory
Shane Cordello was more than just strong muscles and a handsome face—
he was also next in line for the throne of Penwyck. Then, as Shane and his
escort, Sara Wallington, were en route to Penwyck, their plane was hijacked.
And as the danger surrounding them escalated, so did their passion. But upon
their return, could Sara transform the royal prince into a willing husband?

#1475 A Lawman in Her Stocking—Kathie DeNosky
Vowing not to have her heart broken again, Brenna Montgomery moved to
Texas to start a new life—only to find her vow tested when her matchmaking
grandmother introduced her to gorgeous Dylan Chandler. The handsome
sheriff made her ache with desire, but could he also heal her battered heart?

#1476 Do You Take This Enemy?—Sara Orwig
Stallion Pass
When widowed rancher Gabriel Brant disregarded a generations-old family
feud and proposed a marriage of convenience to beautiful—and pregnant—
Ashley Ryder, he did so because it was an arrangement that would benefit
both of them. But his lovely bride stirred his senses, and he soon found
himself falling under her spell. Somehow Gabe had to show Ashley that he
could love, honor and cherish her—forever!

SDCNM1002